DRUMMOND TAKES A HAND

by

Alan Irwin

Dales Large Print Books
Long Preston, North Yorkshire,
BD23 4ND, England.

British Library Cataloguing in Publication Data.

Irwin, Alan
    Drummond takes a hand.

    A catalogue record of this book is
    available from the British Library

    ISBN   978-1-84262-709-9 pbk

First published in Great Britain in 2008 by Robert Hale Limited

Copyright © Alan Irwin 2008

Cover illustration © Gordon Crabb courtesy of Alison Eldred

The right of Alan Irwin to be identified as the author of this
work has been asserted by him in accordance with the
Copyright, Designs and Patents Act, 1988

Published in Large Print 2009 by arrangement with
Robert Hale Limited

Dales Large Print is an imprint of Library Magna Books Ltd.

Printed and bound in Great Britain by
T.J. (International) Ltd., Cornwall, PL28 8RW

DRUMMOND TAKES A HAND

ONE

Jane, wife of homesteader Ed Foster, straightened her back and looked over the patch of vegetable garden which adjoined the house, and which was her pride and joy. She was an attractive fair-haired woman in her late twenties. She had been doing some work in the garden while her husband and young son Davy had taken the buckboard into the nearby town of Danford for supplies.

She looked to the east, through the clear Wyoming air, along the river which ran past the homestead, to see if there was any sign of the returning buckboard. It was not in view, but as she turned to go back into the house, she noticed a rider approaching at a canter from the south. Curious, she waited until the rider, a man, rode up to her, and stopped. He was a stranger to Jane and she took a close look at him.

About five-eleven in height, he was in his early thirties, well-built and clean-shaven. He was neatly dressed, with brown hair showing beneath the brim of his Texas hat. He was wearing a long-barrelled Colt .45 Peacemaker in a right-hand holster. Jane studied his face. A good-looking man, she thought, with a pleasant, open, square-jawed face, and an air of confidence about him. A man who could be trusted, she decided, instinctively.

The stranger touched the brim of his hat.

'Howdy, ma'am,' he said. 'I'm heading for Danford. I'm a stranger in these parts, but I reckon it's somewhere nearby?'

'You reckon right,' said Jane. 'Follow the river for seven miles to the east, and you can't miss it. I'm expecting my husband and boy back from there in the next hour or so. You look like you've had a long ride. I've got a pot of coffee on the stove. Maybe you'd like to share it. Truth is, I couldn't be happier than I am on this homestead, but now and again, I crave to hear a little of what's happening away from here.'

'I'm obliged, ma'am,' said the stranger. 'My name's Drummond, Will Drummond.'

He watered his horse from a trough nearby, then washed his face and hands, using a bowl of water standing near the door of the house. Then he followed Jane inside.

'I'm Jane Foster,' she said. 'I've got a slice of apple pie to go with the coffee. My husband Ed always says that my apple pie was one of the main reasons for him marrying me. Let's see what *you* think.'

During the next half-hour, Will told Jane of a visit he had made to San Francisco about a year earlier, and he described, as best he could, the latest fashions there, at the time, in women's clothing. From her, he learnt that she and her husband and son Davy had moved out West from Illinois three years before, and had laid claim to the quarter-section of 160 acres, on which the house now stood. As she finished speaking, she glanced out of the open window by which they were both sitting, and saw two riders approaching.

'There are two riders heading for the house,' she said. 'I'll go out and see what they want.'

She left the house, and stood outside the door, facing the oncoming riders. As they drew closer, she recognized them as Grant, the burly ramrod of the big Diamond B Ranch which straddled the valley, and Dixon, one of the hands. Each of them was carrying a gun. They stopped on the far side of the garden patch, and Grant asked Jane if her husband was inside.

'He's gone into town,' she replied. 'What

did you want him for?'

'Mr Brent is still waiting to hear that you've accepted that offer he made you in exchange for moving off this homestead,' Grant replied. 'He's getting mighty impatient. He says he's expecting you to move out soon, or face the consequences. Just pass that message on to your husband.'

Jane Foster's face flushed with anger. 'You can tell Brent,' she said, 'that we ain't got no intention of leaving here.'

Grant scowled, and he rode slowly towards the vegetable patch, with the intention of deliberately riding across it. Dixon followed him.

'No!' shouted Jane. 'Keep off my garden!'

Will, who had heard the interchange through the open window, rose quickly and joined Jane outside. The two Diamond B men stopped short of the garden as they saw him appear. They noted the Peacemaker on his right hip.

'Who're you?' asked Grant, looking closely at the stranger.

'A friend of the Fosters,' Will replied. 'You got your answer. I reckon it's time for you to leave. Just turn round right where you are, and ride off.'

Grant hesitated. He felt a strong impulse,

with Dixon's help, to give this meddlesome stranger a lesson.

Will read his mind. 'I don't advise it,' he said. 'Before you could both trigger your guns and fire an accurate shot at me, one, and maybe two of you, would be dead. And the one who's doing all the talking would be my first target. Turn round and leave, and nobody's going to get hurt.'

Grant was seething with anger. But there was something about the look in Will's eye, the expression on his face, and the hand hanging close to the handle of his six-gun that convinced the ramrod to back down.

'We'll be back,' he said, then the two men turned and rode off.

'I sure admire the way you handled those two,' said Jane.

'I've had some practice,' said Will. 'I was a lawman for a spell.'

Jane told Will that the two men who had just left were from the big Diamond B Ranch straddling the valley. The owner, Eli Brent had, for some time, she told Will, been trying to move all the homesteaders out of the valley, so that he could bring more cattle in.

'There are four homesteads along the river, including ours,' she said, 'and Brent has made offers of money to all of us if we leave. But nobody wants to go. We all filed our claims for our quarter-sections, and we figure that, according to the law, nobody can move us off. Trouble is, the nearest lawman is over a hundred miles away.

'We're all pretty worried about the situation. We're wondering what Brent's going to do next. Up to now, he's just been hassling us, without anybody getting hurt. But the way Grant was talking just now, maybe things are going to get worse.'

'Has Brent got any sons?' asked Will.

'We heard that he has one son called Luke,' Jane replied. 'But the rumour is that he's a wanted man, and we've never seen him around here.'

Just then, Jane spotted a buckboard approaching from the east, and they stood outside the house, waiting for it to arrive. Ed Foster looked curiously at Will as he climbed down from the buckboard, followed by his son Davy. Ed was a few years older than his wife. He was a stocky man, of average height, normally cheerful, and with a driving ambition to make a good living out of the homestead. Davy was a boy of nine, who bore a strong resemblance to his father.

Jane introduced Will, then told her husband about the recent visit of Grant and Dixon, terminating with Will's intervention on her behalf.

'I'm sure obliged to you, Mr Drummond,' said Foster. 'I've been afraid something like this might happen. I reckon Brent's set on clearing all us homesteaders out of the valley, whatever it takes. Are you just passing through, Mr Drummond?'

'I figure on staying in Danford for a little while,' said Will. 'I've done a lot of riding lately. Feel like resting up for a spell. It looks like you've picked yourself a good homestead here.'

'We think so,' said Foster. 'It took us a while to find it, but it was worth the effort. There's plenty of water, the soil's good, and we're fairly sheltered in the valley here. Like you see, we have a good-sized corral, and a fenced-in pasture. As well as raising crops, I'm building up a small herd, fenced in, and producing high quality meat. Up to now, things have gone pretty well for us. And the other three homesteads along the river are doing pretty good too.'

Will left the homestead shortly after, and headed for Danford. The Fosters watched him for a while as he rode towards the other homesteads strung along the river bank.

'What d'you make of him, Jane?' asked Ed. 'He sure didn't let out much about himself.'

'I think he's a good man,' she replied. 'He told me he'd been a lawman for a spell, and I believe him. He sure cut Grant and Dixon down to size. I got the feeling that if he had exploded into action, they wouldn't have stood a chance against him. And I'm sure they felt the same way too.'

Will found Danford to be just a small group of buildings, housing the necessary businesses to cater for the needs of the big Diamond B Ranch and the homesteaders. He stopped outside a large building which accommodated a small restaurant and saloon, and also provided sleeping accommodation for the occasional visitor to Danford. He found Fuller, the owner, inside, and enquired about a room for a few days.

'I can fix you up,' said Fuller, a pleasant middle-aged man. 'You got business in town?'

'No,' replied Will. 'Just resting up for a few days.'

As Will was climbing the stairs to his room, he was spotted by Dixon, the Diamond B hand, who had just come in from the street to visit the saloon bar. Will went to the restaurant for supper a little later, then, tired after a long ride, he went back to his room for some sleep.

In the morning, he was just finishing breakfast in the restaurant, when a man walked into the room and up to his table. He was a big man, well dressed and bearded, with an arrogant look about him.

'I'm Brent, owner of the Diamond B,' he said. 'I know you're Drummond, who had a run in with two of my men yesterday. I'd like a word with you.'

Will gestured to the empty chair at the table, and Brent sat down.

'You told my men that you were a friend of the Fosters,' he said, 'but I reckon you can't be all that close, because you're a stranger in the valley, and you ain't staying with them at the homestead. So I figured you might be interested in a proposition I have to put to you.

'You've probably heard that I want the homesteaders out of this valley. I need room for the extra cattle I'm going to bring in. I've been reasonable so far. Offered all of them a good price for moving out and finding homesteads somewhere else. But they're all being obstinate. I need to step up the pressure on them. And that's where you come in. I think you're the kind of man who can throw a real scare into those settlers, for the kind of money I can offer you. And I'm talking *big* money. Are you interested in the job?'

'You wouldn't be bothered if one or two of the homesteaders got killed?' asked Will. 'That might be the only way to get them to move.'

Brent looked hard at the man sitting opposite him. Will's face was expressionless.

'The way I look at it,' said Brent, 'they've only themselves to blame if anything like that happens to them.'

'I was wondering just how far you were prepared to go,' said Will. 'The way *I* look at it, the homesteaders have the legal right to work their homesteads without any inter-ference from you. The solution to your problem seems pretty clear to me. Take your cattle out of the valley, and find some other range that's big enough for the operation you want to run. That would leave the way open for more homesteaders to settle in the valley here.'

Will leaned back in his chair, and awaited the rancher's reaction. Brent rose to his feet, his face flushing with anger.

'I want you out of this valley, Drummond,' he said. 'I don't want you meddling in my affairs. You're only one man. I've got twelve hands on my payroll, and I can bring help in from outside if I need it. Stay on here, and you'll regret it.'

He turned, and stomped out of the restaurant. Fuller, who had seen the rancher and Will at the table, and had heard Brent's raised voice just before he left, came over to speak to Will.

'It looks like you upset Brent,' he said. 'I ain't aiming to pry, just wanted to let you know he's a bad enemy to have. I've had a lot of trouble with his men getting out of hand in here, but I know it's no use complaining to Brent. Sometimes, I wish I'd never started up a business in Danford.'

Will felt sure that Fuller's resentment towards Brent was genuine.

'Has Brent got any family living with him?' he asked.

'None,' Fuller replied. 'I heard that his wife died a while back. And there's a son Luke. I met him only once, in town here, about two years ago. Not long after that I heard a rumour that he was wanted by the law, and as far as I know he ain't been back here since. Which don't mean, of course, that he's never spent any time hiding out on the Diamond B.'

'I expect you know Brent's trying to move

the homesteaders out of the valley,' said Will.

'Yes,' replied Fuller, 'and that's another thing I ain't happy about. The settlers are all good friends of mine. I see hands from the Diamond B in here pretty often, and from what I've overheard, Brent's made his mind up that the settlers have got to leave.'

After getting some information from Fuller about the Diamond B, including the location of the ranch buildings in the valley, Will went to the livery stable for his horse, and rode to the Foster homestead. Ed, working on a repair to the corral fence, saw him coming, and walked to join Jane and Davy, who were working in the garden by the house. When Will reached them, he dismounted at Ed's invitation.

'Howdy,' he said. 'I had a visit from Brent this morning in Danford. Figured you'd like to hear what he had to say. He was offering me a very well-paid job helping him to get you homesteaders out of the valley. When I played along with him for a while, it turned out he would go as far as having some of you killed, if that was the only way to get rid of you. It looks like you and the others are in real trouble. And when I turned Brent down flat, he as good as said I was a dead man if I didn't leave the valley myself.'

'This is bad news,' said Ed. 'I never figured Brent would go that far. We're obliged to you for warning us. I've got to get together with the other homesteaders and talk about this.'

'I'd make it quick,' said Will.

'You're right,' said Ed. 'I'll start on it right now. You'll be leaving the valley, I reckon. No need for you to get mixed up in this affair.'

'I'm already mixed up in it,' said Will. 'I've been ordered by Brent to leave the valley. I don't like threats. I aim to stay and help you homesteaders if that's what you want.'

'We're sure going to be glad of your help,' said Ed. 'You stay here and I'll bring the others back with me. Then we can talk.'

TWO

When Ed Foster had ridden off to round up the men running the other three home-steads, Will had a talk with Jane. He could see that she was deeply worried about the situation.

'It don't seem fair,' she said, 'after all the hard work we've put in here. Brent shouldn't be able to threaten us like this. We like it here, and we own this quarter-section.'

'It's happening in other places where the law is stretched out pretty thin,' said Will. 'All it needs is a greedy rancher who was there first, maybe had some Indian trouble at first, and got round to thinking that the range he was using was all his by right. But maybe we can stop Brent from getting what he wants. I'd like you to tell me about the other homesteaders, before they get here.'

'All right,' said Jane. 'We're pretty friendly with all of them. Starting with the first homestead east of here, that belongs to George and Ruth Bellamy, about the same age as me and Ed. They have a young girl, about eight-years-old. George is a good man, but he has a pretty quick temper. He ain't like Ed. He's liable to act on impulse, without thinking things through.

'Next to them are Andrew and Grace Carter, a few years older than us, with a girl and a boy, ten and eleven years old. Andrew's a quiet man, and a hard worker. Grace does most of the talking.

'The last homestead is run by Hans and Greta Bender. They're a bit older than the rest of us, around fifty, I'd guess. I reckon they'd be the first to think seriously about moving out if Brent started stepping up the pressure.'

Just over an hour later, Ed returned with the three homesteaders. They went into the house and sat down. Ed introduced Will to the others, then spoke to him.

'I've told my neighbours about your conversation with Brent,' he said, 'and they know you were a lawman for a spell. They'll be glad of any advice and help you can give them, but they're wondering if we can come up with the cost of hiring you.'

'I wasn't aiming to get any pay for helping you out,' said Will. 'Food and a bed from one of you is all I need. Brent ordered me out of this valley, which was one sure way of making me stay.'

'That's mighty generous of you,' said Ed. 'You're welcome to stay at our place.'

'Mr Drummond,' said Carter, a short, powerful-looking man, with a placid look about him. 'Ed says you've heard of this kind of thing happening in other places. What do we have to look out for?'

'It varies,' Will replied, 'and the name's Will, by the way. Generally, when the homesteaders have refused any offers of money for moving out, the rancher will start hassling them, first in small ways by getting his hands to ride up to the homesteads and shout insults and threats, and maybe fire off a few shots into the air. If that don't make any difference, the hands may start visiting the homesteads during the night, damaging crops and starting fires. If that don't work, then one or more professional gunfighters might be brought in to pick a fight and kill one of you, to throw a scare into the rest. Another trick is to pick out the homesteader who is most likely to give in under pressure, and concentrate on him. If he leaves, the morale of the others is likely to suffer.'

'So what d'you suggest we do right now?' asked Bellamy.

'Make sure all your weapons are in good

working order,' Will replied, 'and that you have plenty of ammunition. Has each one of you received an offer of money from Brent, in exchange for leaving?'

'Everybody has,' Ed replied, 'from Brent in person. But we all turned him down. And yesterday, before Brent's ramrod Grant was here with Dixon, they had already visited the other three homesteads and got the same answer that Jane gave them. Also, they made the same threats.'

'It seems likely, then,' said Will, 'that Brent's going to get tougher now, and we can expect some night raids on the homesteads, probably attacking one at a time. I know the Diamond B ranch buildings are between the Bender homestead and town. Is there any place between the buildings and the homesteads where a man could hide and see riders heading towards your places during the night?'

'There's just one place,' replied Ed, 'about halfway. It's a small grove of trees that the riders would have to pass close by.'

'Good,' said Will, 'We need some warning of when they're paying us a visit, and we need somebody out in the open when they reach us. We don't all want to have to stay inside all night, wondering whether they're going to turn up, and when and where. But before I go on, is everybody still in favour of standing up to Brent? There's no denying that somebody might get hurt.'

They all nodded, and Will continued.

'What I aim to do myself,' he said, 'is to spend the nights in that grove of trees, watching for riders coming from the Diamond B towards the homesteads. I can get some sleep during the day. I'll follow them, keeping as close as I can in the dark. When I know which homestead they've turned on to, I'll give a warning to you that they're on the quarter-section.'

'How will you do that?' asked Ed.

'I'll agree with each one of you,' Will replied, 'a spot on your homestead which the raiders ain't likely to be going near, and which is about a hundred yards from the house. From that spot, you can run a length of thin, strong wire along the ground to the wall of the house. The spot needs to be marked somehow, so that I can find it in the dark.

'The wire needs to pass through the wall of the house, and inside it's got to be fastened to something so that a pull on the wire by me will make enough of a racket to wake you up. When you get the signal, you can stand by

25

the windows with your weapons, but keep the door fastened on the inside. I'll be out there, checking what they're doing, and firing shots in their direction. If they come near the house, you can fire at them through the windows. Maybe, between us, we can scare them off before they cause any damage. Is there any problem about getting the wire?'

'No,' replied Ed. 'I've got enough for all four homesteads if necessary. Your plan sounds pretty good to me. There's still time to get those wires laid before dark. Did you tell Fuller you weren't going back there tonight?'

'I said I probably wouldn't,' Will replied, 'but I didn't say I'd be staying on one of the homesteads. So Brent won't know where I am, at least for a while.'

Will checked with each homesteader the spot where the end of the wire would be located, and left them to lay it between that point and the house. Arriving back at the Foster homestead, he had a meal with the family, and soon after darkness had fallen he rode off towards the grove, taking some food and drink with him. He had no difficulty finding his hiding place for the night, and tethered his horse well back from the trail.

The night passed without incident, and he

returned to the Foster homestead at day-break. A bunk had been provided for him in the barn, and after telling the Fosters that there had been no sign of Brent's men during the night, he slept there for a few hours.

During the rest of the day, nobody from the Diamond B was seen in the vicinity of the homesteads, and the settlers carried on with their work as usual, none of them going into town. As on the previous day, Will left after nightfall to take up position in the grove.

Shortly after midnight, standing behind a tree just inside the grove, he heard the sound of riders approaching from the east. As they passed him, he could see that there were three of them, riding slowly towards the homesteads. Quickly, he went for his horse, led it out of the grove, then mounted it, and followed the three riders, keeping just out of sight in the darkness. He could hear the faint sound of horses' hoofs meeting the ground, and the occasional sound of voices as the riders talked to one another.

As Will drew near to the point where the track leading to the Bender house led off to the right, he could tell, from the sounds he heard, that the riders had turned on to this track. He followed them, and shortly veered off to his left, and went to the end of the alarm wire, over which a large piece of timber was lying. He dismounted, removed the timber, and pulled as hard as he could on the wire.

Inside the house, the Benders were fast asleep. In the bedroom, the alarm wire was attached to the bottom end of a heavy crowbar leaning against the wall. When Will pulled on the wire, the crowbar clattered down on to the bare timber floor. Instantly awake, the Benders each took hold of a rifle, and stood at one of the windows of the house, watching for any movements outside.

Will left his horse tied to the piece of timber, and cautiously, on foot, he made his way towards the buildings. He circled round them, and came up behind the barn. Looking round the rear corner, he saw the outlines of two figures stealthily approaching the house. He fired several shots towards them, and at the same time Bender and his wife opened fire from the windows. The two intruders stopped short, then ran away from the sources of the shooting, towards their horses. Will, too far away to be seen by the Benders, ran to the front of the barn, and saw a third man come out of the barn door, and run after the others. He sent a shot after him, then noticed a flickering light coming from the interior of the barn. Running inside, he saw that a small pile of hay standing against the timber wall had been ignited, and was now well alight.

Will grabbed a rake, and pulled the burning hay away from the wall, then spread it over the earthen floor. Using a big pail of water standing just inside the door, he doused the flames, making sure they were all properly extinguished. He was certain that had his intervention come more than ten minutes or so later, the timber wall would have caught fire, and the building and its contents would then most likely have been destroyed.

Convinced that the three intruders had left, he quitted the barn. Bender and his wife had stopped firing. Will circled the house at a distance, and ran up to the rear wall, which had no windows. He struck the wall four times with the handle of his six-gun. At this prearranged signal, indicating it was safe to do so, Bender opened the door to let Will in.

Will explained what had happened, and went with Bender to the barn.

'Like you see,' he said, 'you've lost a little hay, is all. It could have been a lot worse. I shot at the man who did it. Winged him, I think. It didn't stop him running off. As for the other two, I don't know whether they were hit or not. They were moving pretty fast when they ran off.'

'We owe you a lot,' said Bender, back in the house. 'What do we do now?'

'You can both go back to bed,' said Will. 'I don't think there'll be any more trouble tonight. But just in case, you'd better rig up your alarm again. I'll go back to the grove until daybreak.'

There was no further sign that night of riders from the Diamond B, and Will returned to the Foster homestead at dawn. He told them what had happened during the night.

'So Brent's stepping up his operation against us,' said Ed. 'Things are getting serious. What do we do now?'

'I think,' Will replied, 'that we should carry on as we are for the time being. There's no doubt in my mind that the three men who rode on to the Bender homestead during the night were from the Diamond B, but we can't prove that. We need to get certain proof that Brent's acting outside the law.'

'All right,' said Ed, 'I'll let the others know.'

Will took some sleep, and in the afternoon he helped Ed with a few jobs around the homestead. After dark, he rode to the grove.

THREE

Will dismounted outside the grove, and led his horse into it. Threading his way through the trees in the darkness, he was suddenly joined by three men, two of whom jabbed the barrels of their six-guns into the small of his back. The third man stood in front of him, and ordered him to put up his hands. From his voice, Will recognized the man as Grant, the Diamond B foreman. Grant took Will's gun, and tied his hands. Then he lit a match, and looked into Will's face.

'We figured it was you, Drummond,' he said. 'You were a fool to join up with the settlers. You should have left the valley when you had the chance. Your luck ran out when you were spotted leaving this grove at daybreak. Mr Brent ain't too happy about one of his men getting shot last night. But you'll be seeing him soon. He'll tell you about that himself.'

One of the hands collected three horses from further inside the grove, then Will was taken to the Diamond B two-storey ranch-house. Grant took him into the living-room, where Brent was waiting. The rancher regarded the prisoner with grim satisfaction.

'You realize now what a fool you were to meddle in my affairs, Drummond,' he said. 'You had your chance to leave. But now you've gone too far. I'm sure you had a hand in wounding one of my men last night.'

'Yes, that was me,' said Will. 'It seemed to me to be the natural thing to do to somebody trespassing and setting fire to somebody else's barn.'

Brent ignored the remark, and spoke to the foreman.

'Put him in that small bedroom upstairs,' he said. 'Tie him up good, and put a guard inside the room with him. Then bring Dixon here.'

In the bedroom, Will was tightly bound, and laid on the bed. A hand sat on a chair near the door. Downstairs, Brent spoke to Grant and Dixon.

'We've got to get rid of Drummond,' he said, 'but not here in the valley. We can't risk being blamed for his death if somebody comes looking for him. I reckon our best plan is to take him out of the valley before daybreak, and fake some sort of fatal accident. And I've got a plan to cover that.

'Before you leave, return all the things we've taken out of his pockets. Then take him out of the valley to Eagle Bluff, and ride to the top of the sheer side. Then throw his body over the edge. Blindfold the horse, then manoeuvre it over the edge as well. After that, ride to the bottom, take the ropes off Drummond, and the blindfold off the horse. Then put Drummond's six-gun on the ground nearby, and come back here.'

Grant and Dixon left with their prisoner three hours before daybreak, and it was still dark when they rode out of the valley. Will was riding his own horse, with his hands tied behind him, and Dixon was leading it. Will was sure that the two men with him had orders to kill him somewhere outside the valley. When dawn broke, he could see that they were riding south towards a tall bluff he could just see in the distance, and which he recollected passing on his way to the valley a few days earlier. He wondered how much further they were going to ride before they reached the spot where he was to die. But there was one glimmer of hope.

Three months previously, Will had been in Amarillo. Before leaving, he had been looking around for a new saddle to replace the one which had given him many years of service, but had reached the end of its useful life. In the livery stable where he had left his horse, he noticed a Denver saddle, in excellent condition, for sale. This, he decided, would suit his purpose, and he asked the liveryman where it came from.

He was told that the saddle had belonged to an outlaw called Nolan, who was shot dead while he and his gang were robbing a bank in Amarillo a couple of weeks earlier. The rest of the gang had escaped,. The saddle had been handed to the liveryman by the law, to cover the cost of bills for stabling which two members of the gang had left unpaid.

Will bought the saddle, and it was on his horse when he left next day on his way to Pueblo, Colorado. He found that it suited him perfectly, and when he stopped for a break at noon, he took a close look at it. He had noticed that the horn at the front of the saddle, and the cantle at the rear, were both thicker than normal. Examining them closely, he noticed that, unusually, there was a small metal knob on top of each.

Curious, he pulled upwards on the knob on the cantle, and a stout blade about three inches long, came slowly into view, before it was prevented from moving out any further. The blade had two sharp cutting edges.

Very ingenious, thought Will. Some saddle maker must have incorporated the blades at the request of Nolan, an outlaw under continuous threat of capture. The blades would provide a chance of escape for a prisoner who, after capture, was being led to jail, on his own horse, and with his hands bound.

When Will rode off from the Diamond B, as prisoner of Grant and Dixon, with his hands tied behind him, his ankles were also tied together with a piece of rope passing under the belly of his mount. Dixon was leading Will's horse, and Grant was riding side by side with Dixon. Will pulled on the knob at the top of the cantle until the blade was fully extended.

Then he started work on the rope holding his two wrists together. The sharp blade made short work of the job, though he suffered a number of cuts on his wrists in the process. Well before they rode out of the valley, his hands were free. But he found that it was impossible to untie the rope holding his ankles together. He would have to wait until they were freed by his captors before making his bid to escape.

When they reached the bluff, and started to climb the sloping side, Will was sure they had arrived at their destination. Reaching the summit, they rode across to the top of the sheer drop to the plain below. Here, Grant and Dixon dismounted, and walked back to Will, who was holding his wrists together behind him, praying that his captors would not immediately check that they were still securely tied. His prayer was answered. Dixon removed the rope between his ankles, and ordered Will to dismount.

Will pulled his feet out of the stirrups, swung his right leg over the neck of his mount, and slid out of the saddle to the ground, his hands still clasped together behind him. As his feet hit the ground, he exploded into action.

Dixon was to his right, only a couple of paces away, and Grant was behind Dixon. Will turned, and moved rapidly towards Dixon, whose gun was plucked from its holster by Will before he realized what was happening. Now without a weapon, he ducked, twisted round, and ran behind the ramrod, who was drawing his six-gun. Will concentrated on Grant, and shot him in the chest. The ramrod's hasty shot missed Will by inches.

Dixon, shielded by Grant, ran to his horse, pulled his rifle from the saddle holster, and turned to face Will, just as Grant collapsed on the ground. Will's second shot hit Dixon in the head before the Diamond B hand had triggered his rifle, and Dixon fell backwards on to the ground. Will walked up to each of his victims to check their condition. Both were dead, lying on the ground about twenty feet back from the top of the sheer face of the bluff.

Will left the horses and the bodies where they were, He was sure that Brent would send men out to look for them when they failed to return, later in the day. He mounted his horse and rode back towards the valley. He waited outside until after dark, then entered it by a route different from the one by which he had been brought out earlier. Once inside the valley, he rode to the Foster homestead, where the family was taking supper.

Ed Foster opened the door to Will's knock. Greatly relieved at the sight of Will, he beckoned him inside.

'We sure are glad to see you,' he said. 'When you didn't turn up this morning, we figured Brent's men must have captured you.'

'That's exactly what happened,' said Will, and went on to tell them about his capture, followed by the attempt to murder him, and his escape, leaving Grant and Dixon dead at Eagle Bluff.

Ed and his wife were clearly shocked by the news.

'So now we know,' said Ed, 'that Brent's ready to commit murder in order to get his own way. I'm sorry you got dragged into this affair. It looks like you were lucky to escape.'

'I wasn't dragged into it,' said Will. 'I have my own reasons for wanting to help you homesteaders. And I figure to carry on doing that, if that's what you want.'

'What's Brent likely to do next?' asked Jane.

'He's lost two men,' said Will, 'and he'll suspect that I'm back in the valley. I think there could be a lull for a few days while he thinks about the situation. He could just back down, and drop the idea of bringing more cattle into the valley. But having met Brent, I think that's unlikely. I think he may bring in somebody from outside to do his dirty work for him. How do you two feel about carrying on the fight against Brent? And how about the others, when they've heard the news?'

'We're here by right,' said Ed, 'and it's a pity the law ain't here to back us up. But we've got roots here now, and I figure this place is worth fighting for. And I think Jane feels the same way.'

He looked at his wife.

'I agree with Ed,' said Jane. 'It's all wrong that we should be forced to leave here just because of one man's greed. I'd been hoping that maybe more homesteaders would turn up so that we could start a school in Danford for the children. After all, the land covered by a quarter-section is nothing compared to the whole of the land in this valley.'

'I'll go and talk with the other homesteaders right now,' said Ed, 'and tell them what's happened, and see how they feel about the situation. But before I go, what do you think we should do for the time being?'

'Carry on as usual, during daylight,' Will replied, 'but keep weapons close by, and watch out for riders from the Diamond B. *I'll* keep watch at night, like I was doing before, but it's clear I can't do it from the grove now. I'll find a place on the Bender homestead where I can watch out for them, whichever homestead they're aiming for. If they turn up, I'll follow them, and raise the alarm like I did before. I might as well go along with you now.'

'All right,' said Ed. 'I see you've still got a six-gun.'

'It belonged to Dixon,' said Will. 'I've got his rifle as well.'

They visited the Bellamys, and the Carters, then went on to the Benders. They told them of Will's capture and escape. All three were still determined to continue to resist Brent's efforts to drive them out of the valley.

Ed returned to his homestead, and Bender took Will to a spot on the homestead, not far from the end of the alarm wire, which was suitable as a look-out position. Bender returned to the house, and Will stayed where he was all night, resisting an almost overpowering desire to sleep, and alternately standing and sitting with his back against a fence post. The night passed slowly but quietly, and he left for the Foster homestead half an hour before dawn. He lay on the bunk in the barn, and was instantly asleep.

When he woke several hours later, Jane gave him a meal in the house. She told him that Ed and Davy had gone into town for supplies. They returned half an hour later, and Ed said that nobody in town had mentioned the deaths of Grant and Dixon, and he had seen no Diamond B hands while he was away from the homestead.

It was the same story over the next four days. There were no sightings of Diamond B men during the day, and no sign of them during the night. Then Carter drove his buckboard back from Danford straight to the Foster homestead. He bore some startling news.

He told his audience that he had just returned from town. While he was standing outside the store, two strangers had ridden in from the south, passing close by him, and he had heard one of them ask a man on the street where the Diamond B ranch-house was located.

'They were both big men,' said Carter, 'with the same bleak look about them. Could be brothers, even twins. They had long faces, and one of them had a scar running down his cheek. They both wore guns, I don't know a lot about professional gunfighters, but that's sure what they looked like to me. They bought a few things at the store, then rode out of town.'

Carter's description of the two men stirred Will's memory. When a lawman, he had studied many Wanted posters describing

41

criminals wanted by the law. On several occasions, he had read a poster describing the twin brothers Bart and Mark Raven. The poster had mentioned a scar on the cheek of one of them.

'I reckon I know who they are,' he said. 'They're the Raven brothers. They're not robbers. They make their money by hiring out to kill people. They're wanted by the law. It looks like Brent's brought them in to do his dirty work.'

'This alters things some,' said Carter. 'How do we deal with the Ravens?'

'The Ravens hire out to kill one or more specified targets,' Will replied. 'Killing is all they do. And I'm certain their first target will be me. Brent will reckon that if I'm killed, you homesteaders will be too scared to stay on here. So I've got to work out some way of getting the better of the Ravens. I think you homesteaders are safe for the time being.'

'If you *are* the first target,' said Ed, 'what can we do to help?'

'I'll let you know later,' Will replied. 'First, I've got some thinking to do. Meanwhile, I suggest all you homesteaders only go into town when it's really necessary, and none of you should go alone.'

When the Raven brothers arrived at the Diamond B ranch house, Brent took them into the living-room, and explained the difficulties he was experiencing in forcing the homesteaders out of the valley.

'Your first job,' he said, 'is to get rid of Drummond. I know he's staying with the Fosters. A couple of days ago he was seen by one of my hands who I'd sent out to watch the homestead through field-glasses. He was helping Foster in one of the fields. He's siding with the homesteaders. Why he's butted in, I don't know. With him gone, I reckon we can soon make the others quit their quarter-sections.'

'This Drummond,' said Bart Raven. 'You say he's killed your ramrod and one of your hands. D'you know anything about him?'

'Nothing,' Brent replied. 'As far as I know, he's never been in the valley before. When we captured him, I figured our biggest problem was solved. Can't understand how he got the better of Grant and Dixon. But one thing's sure. He's pretty handy with a six-gun. Grant was shot through the heart, and Dixon through the head. I figure they both died instantly.'

'We can deal with him,' said Bart Raven.

'What we need to do is think up some way of getting him away from the homesteads, on his own, so that we can ambush him without being seen by anyone but Drummond.'

'All right,' said Brent, 'but don't take too long. I'm ready to start bringing more cows into the valley as soon as the homesteaders have gone.'

FOUR

Late on the afternoon of the day on which the Raven brothers arrived at the Diamond B, a covered wagon rolled into Danford from the south. It was of the type which, since the 1840s, had carried many thousands of pioneers westward over the Oregon trail. The wagon carried Josh Miller and his wife Mary, with their ten-year-old son, Billy. Miller stopped the wagon outside the saloon, where Fuller, the owner, was standing on the boardwalk, looking at them with interest.

'Howdy,' said Miller. 'A friend of ours called Ed Foster has a homestead somewhere in the valley. We'd be obliged if you can tell us where it's located.'

'Sure,' Fuller replied. 'Drive west out of town along the river bank for five miles or so, and you'll reach the homesteads. Ed Foster's is the fourth and last one you come to. Are you folks figuring to settle in the valley?'

'We sure hope we can,' Miller replied. 'We had a letter a while back from Ed, telling us how lucky they'd been to find such a good place in this valley, and how well they'd settled in here. We'd been thinking of heading West, and when the letter came, we decided to join Ed and Jane here. We were pretty close friends back in Illinois. Ran two adjoining farms.'

'Ed and Jane are friends of mine,' said Fuller, 'and I'm sorry to have to tell you that they're having trouble with a rancher called Brent, who's set on running them and the others out of the valley. You'll get the whole story when you see them. The last thing Brent will want to see is another settler turning up to claim a quarter-section in this valley. So I reckon you should wait until after midnight before you drive out to Ed's place. Meanwhile, if anybody asks you, say you're driving north out of the valley in the morning.'

He went on to tell them about the help that Will was giving to the homesteaders. Then Miller thanked him, and drove the wagon to a clear space on the edge of town.

The wagon left at midnight, with Miller and his wife on the seat, and Billy asleep inside. When it reached the Bender homestead, it was heard by Will, in his usual lookout position. He let it pass, then ran up

46

silently behind it. As he drew close, he heard the voices of a man and a woman. He ran up level with the driver, and called on him to stop. Startled, Miller brought the wagon to a halt.

'Sorry to startle you folks,' said Will. 'I'm from one of the homesteads. I'm curious to know what you're doing here.'

'We've travelled from Illinois,' said Miller. 'We're aiming to visit the Fosters. They're old friends of ours.'

'I'd better go with you,' said Will. 'Visitors to the homesteads during the night are liable to get shot at. Follow me.'

Will got his horse, and when they reached the Foster homestead, he told Miller to wait well back from the house, while he went ahead on foot. He approached the rear wall of the house, and struck it four times with the handle of his six-gun. On hearing the pre-arranged signal, Foster let him in. Jane was standing behind him. Will told them that some friends of theirs called Miller, from Illinois, had turned up in a covered wagon, and were waiting to ride up to the house.

'I'll tell them to drive on here,' he said, 'then I'd better go back on look-out.'

Greatly surprised at the news of the arrival of their friends, Ed and Jane ran up to greet them as the wagon stopped outside the house. Leaving Billy asleep in the wagon, the others went inside.

'It's great to see you two,' said Ed. 'When we left Illinois, it looked like we might never see you again. What in blazes made you come out here?'

'It was that letter you sent us,' said Josh Miller, a man in his late thirties, well-built, with a strong rugged face. 'When Mary read how well things had turned out for you here, she started putting the pressure on me to join you.' He smiled at his wife, a plump, pleasant-faced woman of his own age. 'And you know how she can twist me round her little finger. That's why we're here. We did write you before we left, but it seems you never got the letter. We heard in Danford, from a Mr Fuller, that a rancher was trying to get you to leave the valley.'

'That's right,' said Ed, and went on to give the Millers a full account of the situation, including Will's involvement.

'For the time being,' said Ed, 'you'd better stay on our homestead. If we can get Brent to back down, then you could claim a quarter-section just west of ours. Right now, Will's working on a plan to deal with the Raven brothers.'

'Maybe I can help him,' said Josh. 'You know I served in the Union Army back east for a spell, when they were fighting the Confederates.'

'Up to now,' said Ed, 'Will has done all our fighting for us, but now the Raven brothers are here, I reckon he's going to need all the help he can get. But are you sure you want to get mixed up in this?'

'I'm sure,' said Josh. 'We'd like to help, and there's nothing we'd like better than getting to be neighbours of you and Jane in the valley here.'

'We feel the same way,' said Ed. 'Let's all get a little sleep now. When Will gets back, we'll see if he has any plan yet to deal with the Raven brothers.'

Will returned from his look-out position just before dawn, and after sleeping for a few hours, he joined the Fosters and Millers in the house for a meal.

'I've thought up a plan,' he said. 'I think it'll work. But first, can you think of anybody living in Danford who might be in cahoots with the Diamond B outfit?'

'There's just one man I can think of,' Ed replied, 'and that's Penny. He helps out at the store. I've seen him chatting with the Diamond B hands when they're in town.

But we should ask Fuller. He would know.'

'We'll do that,' said Will, and went on to describe his plan.

When he had finished, his audience considered it for a while. Then Josh spoke.

'Sounds good to me,' he said, 'but you can't be thinking of doing the job alone? You need some help. Let me come with you. I've done some fighting in the Union Army, and I'm set on staying on here in the valley.'

'I've got to admit,' said Will, 'that two of us will stand a better chance of pulling it off than me alone. We'll do it together, if you're sure. The first thing to do is ride into town and see Fuller. I reckon he's on the side of the homesteaders. I'm sure we can trust him.' Will and Josh left for Danford shortly after, both carrying arms. They called in briefly at the other homesteads to advise them of the present situation, then rode on into town. They saw nobody on the way. They found Fuller in the saloon. He walked over to them and the three of them sat down at a table. Will asked Fuller if he knew of anybody in town who was on Brent's payroll.

'There's only one man might be,' Fuller replied. 'He's called Penny. Works at the store. I suspect that he keeps Brent advised of anything out of the ordinary happening in town. As a matter of fact, he comes in here every day, regular, and drinks a beer at the bar. He's due in about thirty minutes.'

Taking Fuller into his confidence, Will told him about the deaths of Grant and Dixon, and the arrival of the notorious Raven brothers at the Diamond B.

Startled by the news, Fuller listened intently as Will went on to tell him that he and Josh intended to ambush the Ravens, and that Fuller could, if he was agreeable, help to steer the Ravens into the ambush, without implicating himself.

'I wondered why I hadn't seen Grant and Dixon lately,' said Fuller, 'and I heard about the two strangers turning up in the valley. What is it you'd like me to do?'

Will explained, and Fuller said he would like to cooperate.

'Wait round at the back of the building,' he said, 'and I'll come out and let you know when Penny turns up here.'

Twenty-five minutes later, the saloon-keeper came out, then went back inside. Leaving Josh, Will walked round to the front of the building, and went inside. Fuller was behind the bar, handing a beer to Penny, the only customer standing there. Will walked up to the bar and stood three feet away from

Penny, who recognized him as the man who was helping the homesteaders. Fuller moved along to stand in front of Will.

'I'll have a beer,' said Will.

When Fuller had supplied the drink, Will asked him if he had ever used the telegraph office in a small town called Lantry, about fourteen miles to the south, through which Will had passed on his way to the valley.

'Sure,' Fuller replied. 'It's the nearest telegraph office to Danford. I use it now and again.'

'I want to ride in there around noon to-morrow,' said Will, 'to send a telegraph message. Will the office be open then?'

'Tomorrow, it'll be open all day,' Fuller replied.

As he continued chatting with Will on other topics, Fuller noticed that Penny was drinking his beer at a much faster rate than was his normal custom. Immediately his glass was empty, he walked quickly out of the building.

Ten minutes later, Josh came in, having completed his task of watching Penny's actions on leaving the saloon.

'He went straight to the livery stable,' said Josh, 'came out with a saddled horse, and rode off fast in the direction of the Diamond

B ranch-house.'

'It looks like he could have taken the bait,' said Fuller. 'I've been thinking about the spot the Ravens would be most likely to use for an ambush. The only place I can think of on the trail between here and Lantry is the canyon about four miles north of there.'

'We figured the same as you,' said Will, his mind on a spot halfway through the canyon, where the ground near the walls was studded with large boulders, with a bend in the canyon just south of this. 'The canyon is where we aim to surprise them. They'll be expecting me to ride through there not long before noon tomorrow.'

Will and Josh returned to the Foster homestead, and shortly after nightfall, they rode out of the valley, and headed for the canyon. Each of them was armed with a six-gun and a rifle. When they reached the canyon, they rode past the boulders, ideal hiding places for a lethal ambush at close range, and round the bend, then on to the end of the canyon, where they tethered their horses, out of sight of the trail. They walked back through the canyon, and found a recess in the wall, seventy yards south of the bend, from which, concealed, they could look along the canyon for riders approaching from the north.

Here they stayed, taking a few hours sleep in turn, until a little before dawn, when they both moved up to the bend, and found a place from which they could see any riders from the north approaching them.

'We'll wait here till we see them coming,' said Will. 'Remember, Josh, these men are real killers. It's their job. It's all they do. If we can surprise them, and take them prisoner without any gunplay, we'll do that. Otherwise, if we want to stay alive, we've got to shoot to kill.'

'All right,' said Josh. 'I understand. I'll do the best I can.'

When Penny arrived at the Diamond B with the news of Will's intention to go to Lantry the following morning, the Ravens immediately decided that this provided them with an excellent chance of eliminating Will. Having recently followed the trail from Lantry to Danford themselves, they immediately seized on the canyon as an ideal place for the ambush. They decided to time their arrival there for just after dawn, when they would find a suitable place for the ambush, and would await Drummond's arrival.

Will and Josh did not have to wait long

before they saw the Ravens approaching. They went back to the recess where they had spent the night, and stood looking towards the bend. Ten minutes later, the Ravens appeared in view as they rode round the bend, dismounted, and tethered their horses close to the canyon wall. Then they disappeared from view, on foot, in the direction from which they had come.

Will and Josh waited for a few minutes, then walked up to their previous position at the bend. They could see that the Ravens, awaiting the arrival of a rider from the north, had taken up position behind a boulder, about five feet high, near the wall on the opposite side of the canyon. Behind the outlaws was another boulder, larger in size.

'What we'll do, Josh,' said Will, 'is wait till around the time those two will be expecting me to turn up. Then we'll cross the canyon, and make our way round the bend and along the wall to that big boulder behind the Ravens. We can use it as cover. Then we'll have a good chance of creeping up behind them, and taking them prisoner.'

When they left their position, an hour and a half before noon, the Ravens were both standing, looking along the canyon over the top of the boulder. Moving quietly, Will and

Josh reached the boulder behind the outlaws without being observed. Will peered round it. Both the Ravens were standing with their backs to him, looking intently along the canyon. Their six-guns were in their holsters, and their rifles were on the ground close by. Will whispered to his companion, then, holding their six-guns, they both came out from behind the boulder.

Moving as silently as possible, they tiptoed, side by side, towards the two outlaws, Will heading for Bart Raven, Josh for his brother Mark. But they were less than halfway there when Josh stepped on a loose piece of rock, and stumbled. Hearing the sound, the brothers twisted round, reaching for their six-guns. Will shot Bart Raven in the chest, and the shot from the outlaw, who fired just after he was hit, went wide. Mark Raven, slower to react than his brother, saw Josh who, losing his balance, had fallen on the ground. Desperately, Josh sought to rise to his feet, as Mark Raven brought his six-gun to bear on him. But an instant before the outlaw was ready to trigger his gun, Will's second shot took him in the chest. Both outlaws collapsed on the ground, and lay motionless. As Will stepped forward to check them over, Josh rose shakily to his feet.

'They're both dead,' said Will. 'You all right?'

'Thanks to you, I am,' Josh replied. 'For a few seconds there, I figured I was a goner. What do we do now?'

'Let's look through their pockets and saddlebags first,' said Will.

On doing this, the only item of interest they found was a letter, signed by Brent, and addressed to Bart and Mark Raven, which had obviously been delivered by hand. It requested the Ravens' urgent help in ridding the Diamond B of a meddlesome stranger who was obstructing Brent's plans for expanding his operation in the valley.

'We'll keep this,' said Will, 'and we'll bury the bodies at the side of the canyon. There's plenty of loose bits of rock around to cover them up with. Then we'll turn the Ravens' horses loose, and go back to the valley.'

They reached the Foster homestead without encountering anyone from the Diamond B. Greatly relieved to see them, Josh's wife and the Fosters were told that the Ravens no longer presented a threat to the homesteaders. Ed rode off to give the news to the others.

When Ed returned, he sat down with Josh and Will to discuss the new situation.

'I don't know what Brent'll do,' said Will, 'when he realizes that I'm still alive, and that there'll be no more help coming from the Raven brothers. He might give up, or he might call in some more help. We'll just have to wait and see.'

'You'll be staying on for a while?' asked Ed.

'I think there's something I should tell you now,' said Will, 'but I'd like it kept between the three of us. Up to six months ago, I was a sheriff in Kansas. One of my deputies was my young brother Clint. He was out on a routine mission, when he rode, by chance, into the camp of a couple of outlaws who had, unbeknown to him, robbed a stage-coach the previous day, in an adjoining county.

'They got the drop on him, and out of pure evil, seeing he was a lawman, one of them shot him deliberately through the palm of each hand, then in the chest, and they left him for dead. He was found by two ranch hands, barely alive, and before he died, he told them what had happened. He said that after being captured, he had recognized the man who shot him as the man on a Wanted poster he had seen recently. The man was Luke Brent.'

'The son of Brent of the Diamond B?' said Ed.

'That's right,' said Will. 'I quit my job, and started out on a search for Luke Brent. But I had no luck. No sightings of him were reported. It seemed like he'd just vanished. I'd heard that his father ran a ranch here, and in the end, I decided to come here, and hang around in the hope that Luke Brent would turn up sometime. So I aim to stay on in the valley for a while yet. Maybe I can help out with the work on the homesteads.'

'I can't say I ain't happy you'll be around for a while,' said Ed. 'You're welcome to carry on staying with us.'

When the Raven brothers did not return to the Diamond B, Brent sent two men to the canyon. They found the two graves and, not far away, the Ravens' horses. They returned to the ranch, to pass on the bad news to Brent. Shortly after their return, a ranch hand, sent to observe the Foster homestead through field-glasses, reported seeing Will, and three other newcomers to the valley – a man, woman and a boy. And he reported seeing a covered wagon standing near the house.

FIVE

During the seven weeks following the demise of the Ravens, there was no sign that Brent was continuing his efforts to drive the homesteaders out of the valley. Josh pegged out a 160-acre quarter-section next to the Foster homestead, and moved the wagon on to it. Then he started on the process of building the house, ordering materials through the general store in Danford. When these started to arrive by freight wagon, Will gave a hand as the building of the house began.

Then, from Fuller, in town, Will heard the news that four riders had turned up at the Diamond B. And one of them was Luke Brent.

'I heard the news from a Diamond B hand in the saloon,' said Fuller. 'He was pretty drunk at the time, and before he could say any more, another hand who was with him, took him out of the saloon. I've been wondering whether Luke and the others are here to help Eli Brent to clear the valley of homesteaders.'

'It's possible,' said Will. 'When I get back, I'll tell all the homesteaders to be on their guard. Then we'll just have to wait and see. If you happen to hear just why those four have turned up at the Diamond B, we'll all be mighty obliged if you'd let us know.'

'I'll do that,' said Fuller. 'I heard that Miller has filed his claim for a quarter-section.'

'That's right,' said Will. 'Once he's lived on it and farmed it for five years, the land is his.'

The following day, Ed decided he needed to go into Danford for supplies. He set off on the buckboard, accompanied by the two boys, Davy and Billy, who had become firm friends since the Millers arrived in the valley. Their departure from the Foster homestead was observed by a Diamond B hand who was keeping watch on the homestead through field-glasses.

Immediately, the hand rode off to tell Eli Brent that Foster, accompanied by two boys, was heading towards town on a buckboard. Five minutes later, a buckboard left the Diamond B, with two men on board, heading for Danford.

When Ed Foster arrived in town with the boys, he went inside the store, and sat down waiting while another customer was being served. Outside the store, Davy and Billy were sitting on the edge of the boardwalk, observing the small amount of activity that was all Danford had to offer. They saw a man walk out of an alley between two buildings on the opposite side of the street. The man was a stranger to Davy. He stopped in front of them.

'You boys like to earn a bit apiece?' he asked.

'What do we have to do?' asked Davy.

The man pointed along the street.

'You see the last shack on the right,' he said. 'Behind it is my partner, waiting for me with a buckboard. All I want you to do is tell him I got held up, and it'll be half an hour before I can join him.'

It was too tempting an offer for the boys to resist. They nodded in unison, and he handed a bit to each of them. Then, as the two boys started running along the street, he went back through the alley, and ran along the rear of the buildings, in the same direction as the boys.

When Billy and Davy reached the shack, and went round to the back, they found a buckboard there, with a man standing by it. He also was a stranger to Davy. Like the man who had sent them on the errand, he was powerfully built, was armed with a pistol, and did not have the appearance of a ranch hand.

Davy passed the message to the man, and as he was finishing, the boys were surprised to see the stranger they had just left appear on the scene. Before they realized what was happening, they were grabbed by the two men, overpowered, and bound and gagged. Then they were laid on the buckboard, and covered with a canvas sheet. The two men climbed on to the seat, and the buckboard was driven away from town to the west. As far as the two men were aware, their capture of the two boys had remained unnoticed.

It was some time before Ed obtained all his supplies, and was ready to leave. But there was no sign of the two boys. At first annoyed, then increasingly concerned, he searched the town, outside the buildings. Then he checked all the buildings themselves. His search attracted attention, and Fuller and the storekeeper helped him to make a further exhaustive search which was no more successful than the previous ones.

Nobody in town had seen any strangers or Diamond B hands around, and the only possible clue as to what had happened to the boys was that a woman hanging out some washing at the time that Ed was in the store, had seen a buckboard some way out of town. Two men were on the seat, and the buckboard was moving away from town in a westerly direction. The men were too far away for her to recognize or describe.

'There's nothing more I can do here,' said Ed despairingly. 'I'm going back to tell the others what's happened, and see what Will thinks about the situation.'

When Ed arrived back at the homestead, he told Jane, Will and the Millers the distressing news, and Will suggested that all the homesteaders should assemble at the Foster homestead, to discuss this grave turn of events which was causing such concern, particularly to the Fosters and Millers.

When the homesteaders had all arrived, Will spoke to them. They were all now aware that initially, he had come to the valley in the hope of catching up with outlaw Luke Brent, his brother's killer. He said that he suspected that Luke Brent and the three men who had arrived with him were now helping Eli Brent in his bid to drive the homesteaders out of the valley. It seemed likely, he told them, that the boys had been hidden on the buckboard seen leaving the area, and his own opinion was that Luke Brent was behind their disappearance.

'It's the sort of thing he would do,' said Will. 'He has no scruples.'

'If what you think is true,' said Jane, 'is he going to harm Davy and Billy?'

'Not right away, I'm sure,' said Will. 'But my guess is that he's going to threaten to do that unless all you homesteaders leave the valley. In which case, we should be hearing from the Diamond B pretty soon. I reckon that we've no option but to wait and see what they have to say. Then we can all talk it over, and decide what our next move is to be. Our main aim has got to be to get the boys back without any harm coming to them.'

The homesteaders discussed the matter, and decided to do as Will had suggested. They did not have long to wait before the approach from the Diamond B. They had all just left the house at the end of the meeting when they saw four riders approaching from the east. The riders headed straight for the house, and stopped a few yards from Will and the homesteaders. Immediately, Will recognized one of the four armed men as Luke Brent. He had never met him face to face, but he had seen him portrayed on

Wanted posters.

The face Will was looking at was a cruel, arrogant one, made even more unattractive by an habitual sneer. Will resisted a strong impulse to gun him down on the spot. He looked at the three riders with the outlaw. All were tough-looking characters, strangers to the valley. All had the same aggressive look about them as their leader.

Luke Brent looked closely at the group of people standing in front of him.

'I guess one of you is Drummond,' he said.

'That's me,' said Will. 'What's your business here?'

Brent grinned evilly. 'It's just a friendly call,' he said. 'We figured you might be worried about two of your boys going missing in Danford. We rode out specially to let you know they turned up safe and sound on the Diamond B. Just now, they're being took good care of, but how long that goes on depends on you homesteaders.'

'What do we have to do?' asked Will.

'Just leave the valley,' Luke Brent replied. 'It's as simple as that. And we ain't going to be unreasonable. We're not asking you to move out today or tomorrow. You can stay here until a week from today. On that day you'll all move out together, and we'll have the boys waiting for you some place outside the valley. We'll let you know where that place is on the day you leave. And let me tell you right now. The boys ain't being held on the Diamond B. They're not inside the valley.

'We're pretty sure you folks will see reason. But if you don't, and try to bring help in from outside, you'll never see those boys again. So one week from today, in the morning, we'll be here to escort you all out of the valley, and once we're well clear of it, we'll tell you where you can pick up the boys. I reckon that's all I have to say to you right now.'

The four riders wheeled their mounts, and rode off, leaving consternation behind them.

'D'you think that threat about us never seeing the boys again is just a bluff?' a deeply worried Jane asked Will.

'Knowing Luke Brent's history,' Will replied, 'I'd say the threat is probably a real one.'

'It looks like none of us has any option,' said Carter. 'It's clear to me that if we can't get the boys back unharmed before the date we've been given to leave, then we'll have to move out.'

All the homesteaders expressed agreement

with this view. Then Will spoke.

'The problem is,' he said, 'that's hard to plan a rescue when we've no idea just where the boys are. I'm going to town first thing in the morning to see if Fuller has heard anything about the boys' whereabouts. He might have overheard something in the saloon.'

Will rode into Danford early the following day, and went to see Fuller, who took him into a small private room behind the bar. Fuller listened as Will told him about the visit of Luke Brent and his men to the Foster homestead the previous day.

'Brent has gone too far this time,' said Fuller. 'I suppose all the settlers are going to leave?'

'Unless we can rescue the boys,' Will replied. 'I don't suppose you've got any idea where they're being held?'

'No, I haven't,' Fuller replied, 'but if there's any way I can help you, let me know.'

'I've just had the glimmering of an idea,' said Will. 'Does Eli Brent often come into town?'

'Not often,' Fuller replied, 'but there *is* one regular visit he makes. And that's to have new shoes fitted on that big palomino he rides. He's mighty proud of that horse. Won't let anybody else ride it. And it so happens he's bringing it in for shoeing tomorrow morning, so my friend Wes Haley, the blacksmith, tells me. Wes is a good friend of mine, and he feels the same way as I do about the way the homesteaders are being treated.'

'Does Eli Brent usually ride in alone?' asked Will.

'Sometimes, but not always,' Fuller replied. 'Now and then, his ramrod would ride in with him.'

'I think,' said Will, 'that I can see a way of getting the boys back, if the blacksmith is willing to give us a little help. I can see that he wouldn't want Eli Brent to know that he was helping the homesteaders, and I think that could be arranged.'

'Wait here,' said Fuller. 'I'll go for Wes, and bring him in the back way. Then you can tell him what you have in mind.'

Fuller returned with the blacksmith ten minutes later, and Will told them of the plan he had in mind.

'I'll be glad to help you out with that,' said Haley. 'In fact, I'm looking forward to it. Eli Brent usually turns up with his palomino around nine in the morning.'

They discussed the details of Will's plan, then Haley left, followed a few minutes later by Will, who took a good look at the inside of the blacksmith's shop, then returned to the Foster homestead. On the way, he stopped at each of the three homesteads, told them of his plan, and asked them to stock up with supplies that day, from the store in Danford. He repeated this request to Ed and Josh later, when he told them about his plan.

Early the following morning Will, accompanied by Josh, drove a buckboard into Danford, and proceeded to the rear of the blacksmith's shop. They climbed down and, carrying some rope, they went inside, where Haley greeted them. They were both armed. The blacksmith hung a notice on the outside of the doors, indicating that the shop was closed until noon. Then he went back inside, closing the doors behind him. Will and Josh stood by a window which gave a view of the trail coming in from the west. It was well over an hour later when two riders came into view, one of them astride a big palomino.

Will called to Haley, who came over to look.

'That's Eli Brent all right,' he said. 'Couldn't mistake that horse. But who's the rider with him? I can't tell at this distance.'

The man was, in fact, Garner, one of the

three men Luke Brent had brought with him, and a distant relative of his. As the two riders drew closer, Will and Josh recognized Brent's companion as one of the men accompanying Luke Brent on his recent visit to the Foster homestead.

'He's one of Luke Brent's men,' said Will.

'I'd better be moving,' said Haley, and he left the premises, removing the notice, and pulling the two big swing doors together behind him before going to his house next door. Josh and Will each took up a position behind one of the doors.

It was not long before they heard the sound of the approaching riders. Eli Brent and Garner dismounted, pushed open the doors, and went into the shop, walking side by side. Before they realized what was happening, each of them felt the end of a gun barrel jammed into the small of his back. They came to an abrupt stop as their six-guns were removed and dropped on the floor. The two men were pushed up against a wall, and Will kept them covered while Josh tied their hands behind them. Josh closed the two doors, and the prisoners were ordered into a store room at the back of the shop. Josh pushed the door to behind them.

Eli Brent was seething with anger. 'Damn

you, Drummond,' he said,. 'You've made a big mistake. You'll never get away with this.'

'We'll see,' said Will, as he forced a gag into the rancher's mouth, and secured it in position.

Quickly, Garner was gagged as well, and both prisoners were tightly bound and laid on the floor.

'Before we take them out,' said Will, 'I'll make sure there's nobody around.'

He walked towards the door of the storeroom, then stopped as he heard sounds outside. He gestured to Josh, and they stood behind the door. A moment later, Haley pushed it open and walked in. His jaw dropped at the sight of the two men lying on the floor. Then he put up a strong resistance as Will and Josh took hold of him from behind, and wrestled him to the floor. But it was futile. A few minutes later, he was lying, bound and gagged, close to the other two prisoners.

Josh put the CLOSED notice back on the doors leading into the street, and went out of the rear door to check that there was no one around. Then he and Josh dragged out Eli Brent and Garner, one by one, lifted them on the buckboard, and covered them with a canvas sheet. Will returned briefly to release Haley, then he and Josh climbed on to the buckboard, and headed for the homesteads, while Haley, unobserved, led the prisoners' horses to the rear of the blacksmith's shop, where they would be out of sight.

As Will and Josh passed by each homestead, aware that the settlers would be on the lookout for them, they gave a prearranged signal to indicate that they were carrying Eli Brent on the buckboard. When they arrived at the Foster homestead, the prisoners were put in the barn, with Josh guarding them for the time being.

There was considerable activity at the three homesteads receiving the signal, and it was not long before a buckboard carrying supplies, and accompanied by a small number of livestock, left each one of them, and proceeded to the Foster homestead. Here they settled down to help guard the prisoners, and await the next phase of Will's plan.

Will had completed a letter to Luke Brent, and had shown it to the homesteaders. It was addressed to the outlaw, and read: 'We are holding your father and one of your men at the Foster homestead. Your father will be exchanged for the two boys you kidnapped.

If you refuse to exchange, your father will suffer. The same applies if you try to rescue him, or cause any damage to the home-steads. We will communicate only through Penny alone. Anybody turning up here from the Diamond B, without our permission, will be shot. Drummond.'

Will handed the letter, in a sealed enve-lope, to Bellamy, who had volunteered to take it to Penny, in town, for him to deliver to Luke Brent at the ranch.

'Take my horse,' said Will. 'I reckon it's the fastest one we have. Ride as quick as you can into town, and do the same coming back. We don't want to run the risk of you being captured by anybody from the Dia-mond B.'

When Bellamy reached Danford, he found Penny leaving the store, in which he had been working all morning. He showed him the envelope, and asked him to take it to Luke Brent.

'We know you do work for Eli Brent,' he said. 'This is mighty urgent. Needs to be taken right away. You'll be in real trouble with Brent if you don't do what I say.'

Bellamy handed the letter to Penny, and rode fast out of town. Penny followed him a few minutes later. The arrival and departure of Bellamy, and the departure of Penny were closely observed by Haley, who had hidden in the blacksmith's shop since Will and Josh had left on the buckboard.

Haley left the blacksmith's shop and ran to the saloon, where he told Fuller and the few customers inside about the capture of Eli Brent and Garner by Will and Josh, who had left him, tied up and gagged, in his shop.

'I've only just freed myself,' he said. 'I wonder where they've taken their prisoners.'

'It's no concern of ours,' said Fuller. 'I guess we'll hear soon enough about what's happening.'

SIX

Penny found Luke Brent in the Diamond B ranch-house. He handed him the envelope. As the outlaw read the letter, his face suffused with rage. He handed the letter to Penny, and waited while he read it.

'You knew nothing of this?' he asked.

'No, I didn't,' Penny replied. 'I was in the store all morning. Didn't see a thing. This letter was handed to me by Bellamy, one of the homesteaders, about half an hour ago. He didn't tell me what was inside it. Just said to get it to you as quick as I could. Then he rode off towards the homesteads.'

'Damnation!' said Brent. 'We'll have to make the exchange. There's no option. You ride to the Foster homestead, and tell Drummond we'll make the exchange before dark. Say I'll bring the boys to a point about a hundred yards from the house. I'll be alone, except for them. Then, when Drummond fires his gun in the air, both my father and the boys will start walking towards each other. See if Drummond agrees to this.

Then ride back here and wait for me. I'm going to pick up the boys from outside the valley. Shouldn't be more than a couple of hours.'

Penny rode to the Foster homestead. He was greeted by the sight of all the settlers, carrying weapons, standing near the house, awaiting his arrival. He saw Will, and stopped a few yards in front of him. He passed on Luke Brent's message.

'Tell Luke Brent we agree,' said Will. 'We'll do it the way he suggests. But if there's any trickery, his father will suffer for it.'

'I'll tell him that,' said Penny. He wheeled his horse, and headed for the ranch-house.

Jane and Mary walked up to Will.

'Are we really going to get Davy and Billy back soon?' asked Jane.

'I think we are,' Will replied. 'I can't see what could go wrong.'

An hour before nightfall, Luke Brent was seen riding towards the homestead, accompanied by two boys sitting on another horse. They all dismounted about a hundred yards from the house, and the outlaw told the boys that when he gave the word, they were to walk, not run, to their parents.

Will confirmed the identities of the two boys through field-glasses. Eli Brent was

78

brought out of the barn, his legs now freed. Will fired his gun in the air, and the boys and the rancher started walking towards each other. When the boys reached the group of settlers, and were found to be unharmed, there was great rejoicing. Will watched the Brents until they disappeared from view in the direction of the ranch-house. Then he spoke to the homesteaders.

'We've still got one of Luke Brent's men to bargain with,' he said, 'but maybe that won't stop them attacking this homestead. So we need to make sure that we're ready for them any time they decide to try, though I doubt if they'll do anything tonight. And we've got to keep a close guard on the prisoner. I guess some of you are worried about not being able to tend your crops, but I reckon we have a much better chance of getting the better of Brent if we all stay together for the time being.'

This proposal was agreed by the homesteaders, and Will went on to discuss the arrangements for guarding the homestead.

'Between nightfall and dawn,' he said, 'I think we should all stay in the house, including the prisoner. I know it'll be crowded, but I reckon we ain't got no choice. And to give us warning of a attack from any direction during the night, I think we should rig up an alarm system, first thing tomorrow morning. I expect Brent will have a man watching us, but he'll be too far off to understand exactly what we're doing.

'What I have in mind is a wire circling the group of buildings, and running, just above ground level, through holes in stakes driven hard into the ground. The wire will be divided into six sections, and each section will be connected to another wire running through the wall of the house. Inside the house, each wire will pull on something which will give an alarm, so that we'll know in which direction they're coming from. And since this house has a window in each wall, a rifle at each window can cover attacks from all directions.'

'I reckon that's a good idea,' said Josh. 'We've got the wire, and the timber for the stakes. We'll start on it at daybreak.'

Will went on to suggest that this might be a good time to try and get the law to give them some help. 'I know there's a US marshal in Denver called Harper. He's a federal officer. I met him a few times when I was a sheriff. He's a good man. I reckon we should send him a telegraph message from Lantry, telling him that Luke Brent, with two of his men, is in the valley, at his father's Diamond B Ranch, and that he's holding us under siege, on the Foster homestead, where we're holding the fourth member of his gang. I'll ask him to get help to us as soon as he can. I think I can rely on him to respond, because Luke Brent is wanted for robbery and murder in three or four states. But it may take a while before he can get some law officers here. Meanwhile, we've got to hold out the best we can.'

'When do we send the message?' asked Ed. 'I'm volunteering to take it to Lantry. It's clear *you* can't be spared from here yourself.'

'All right,' said Will. 'You'll leave here in the morning, two hours before dawn. Hand the message in at the telegraph office around noon, and don't ride back into the valley until after dark. Don't touch the alarm wires, and give the agreed knock on the wall of the house when you reach it.'

There was no sign of intruders during the night, and Ed departed as planned. He rode into Lantry just before noon, and dismounted outside the telegraph office. He tied his horse to the hitching-rail, already occupied by one other mount.

Earlier that day, on the Diamond B, Luke Brent had prepared a telegraph message to send to a friend of his called Curtis, the leader of a gang of outlaws hiding out near Amarillo in the Texas Panhandle. Curtis was expecting Luke Brent and his men to join up with his gang in the near future, to carry out a robbery involving a large shipment of gold by Wells Fargo. The message was to tell Curtis that the arrival of Luke Brent and his men would be delayed.

The message was taken to Lantry by Arnold, one of Luke Brent's men. He arrived at the telegraph office not long before noon, and went inside. The operator was busy receiving some messages, and Arnold stood waiting until he finished. Then he waited while his own message was transmitted. He was just about to leave when, through the window, he saw a rider come up to the hitching-rail, and dismount. He looked familiar, and Arnold suddenly realized that he had seen him among the group of homesteaders when Luke Brent had told them of the capture of the two boys. Arnold came up behind the operator, pistol-whipped him over the head, and lowered his body to the floor. Then he stood beside the door.

Ed took the message out of his pocket,

opened the door of the office, and stepped inside. As he saw the operator lying on the floor, he felt the barrel of a six-gun pressed into the middle of his back. His own six-gun was taken from its holster, and the message was taken out of his hand.

'We're taking a ride to the Diamond B,' said Arnold, glancing out of the window, where the street appeared to be empty. 'Go outside in front of me, and get on your horse. Then ride out of town ahead of me. Do anything foolish, and I'll gun you down.'

Ed had recognized Arnold as one of Luke Brent's men, and he figured that any attempt on his part to escape was bound to fail. Cursing the misfortune which had brought him to the telegraph office at the same time as his captor, he rode on in silence until they reached the Diamond B ranch-house. Luke Brent came out of the house as they reached it. He recognized Ed as one of the home-steaders.

'This is a stroke of luck,' he said. 'Now we can get Garner back. How in blazes did you manage to capture him?'

'It was in Lantry,' said Arnold, 'just after I'd sent your message to Curtis. He turned up to send a telegraph message, but I got the drop on him before he could send it. I've

83

got it here.'

He handed the message to Luke Brent, who read it with mounting concern.

'If this had gone,' he said, 'we could have been in serious trouble. We've got to see that they don't get another chance to send this message.'

He went to discuss the matter with his father, and half an hour later, he rode towards the Foster homestead with Ed as his prisoner. They were spotted when they were some distance away, and Will went to a point well away from the house, out of sight of the alarm wires, to wait for them. Luke Brent and his prisoner stopped when they were in hearing distance of Will, who had recognized Ed, and was wondering how he had come to be captured. Luke Brent called out.

'You can see I've got one of your friends here, Drummond,' he said. 'I figured you might like to exchange Garner for him.'

'All right,' said Will. 'You move back seventy yards, and I'll bring Garner to where I'm standing now. I'll fire my gun like before, and they can both start walking.'

Will went for Garner in the barn, and led him back, blindfolded, to the spot from which he himself had been speaking to Luke

Brent earlier. He took the blindfold off, and the exchange took place. The two outlaws rode off, and Ed and Will returned to the house. On the way Ed told how he had been captured before he had been able to send the message to Curtis.

'I saw Luke Brent read the message,' he said, 'and I could see he was mighty relieved it hadn't been sent.'

'This means,' said Will, 'that they'll do everything they can to stop us sending another message.'

In the house, Will discussed the present situation with the men, while Jane and Mary kept a watch outside for approaching riders.

'The Brents will be aiming to make sure,' said Will, 'that no telegraph message gets through to the US marshal. I'm sure they're keeping watch on us during the day. I reckon that from now, during the night, they'll have a ring of men around the house, but well back from it, to stop any rider leaving. And I guess it won't be long before they decide to attack the house, now they've got Garner back.'

'So all we can do,' said Josh, 'is do our best to hang on here until our supplies run out?'

'Not quite,' said Will. 'Fuller, in town, told me he was willing to help us any way he could, and I know he goes to Lantry now and again, to send telegraph messages. I reckon that if we got our message to him, he'll take it there for us.'

'That's fine,' said Josh, 'but how do we get it to him?'

'A rider would never get through to Danford,' said Will, 'because a rider is what they'll be looking out for. But a man on foot would stand a good chance. You've seen how low the river is just now. The bank on both sides, for well over a mile from here towards town, is over two feet high, and right now the water doesn't come up to the foot of the bank. A man could crouch down there, and move along without being seen. As soon as it's properly dark, I'll leave. Should be back long before dawn.'

'Not a good idea,' said Josh. 'You're needed here. We don't know what might happen during the night. I'll take the message to Fuller myself.'

'All right,' said Will. 'I'll write it out again for you.'

Josh set out an hour after nightfall. The sky was overcast, and visibility was low. He jumped down to the bed of the river, crouched down, and moved along the bank towards Danford. The night was still, and as he progressed, the only sound he could hear, faintly, was that of his footsteps along the bed of the river. Then he froze as he heard a man's cough, a little way from the river. As he waited there, the cough was repeated, then there was silence. Cautiously, he continued along the river bed until he had covered a further mile. Then he climbed to the top of the bank, and headed along it, towards town.

He reached Danford before midnight and, keeping off the street, he went to the rear of the saloon, and tapped on the window of Fuller's private room behind the bar. Luck was with him. Fuller opened a door not far from the window, and Josh walked up to it. Recognizing the man outside, Fuller beckoned him in, and took him to his room.

'I've been wondering,' said Fuller, 'what's been happening on the homesteads.'

Josh related to the saloon-keeper events which had occurred since he and Will had taken Eli Brent and Garner prisoner in Danford.

'Will figured,' said Josh, 'that you might be willing to help us by getting the telegraph message to Marshal Curtis sent from Lantry. He reckons that the marshal will be keen to get his hands on Luke Brent and his gang.'

'I can do that for you,' said Fuller. 'Everybody knows that I use the telegraph office in Lantry now and again. I'll take the message there tomorrow morning. And I'm hoping you folks manage to hold out till help gets here.'

'We're obliged to you,' said Josh, and handed the message over. 'I'd best be getting back now.'

Josh left by the rear door, and retraced his steps, dropping to the bed of the river at the same point at which he had left it earlier. Then he moved towards the Foster homestead. He was approaching the point from which he had earlier heard the sound of coughing, when suddenly, without warning, a man dropped down from the top of the bank several yards in front of him, and filled a mug with water from the river. The outline of the man, against the night sky, was just visible to Josh, and he pressed himself hard against the bank, and crouched there, motionless.

The man stood there for a while, looking across the river. Then he climbed back to the top of the bank, and sat down, with his legs hanging over the edge. Josh stayed motionless, fearing that any movement on his part would attract the attention of the man seated nearby. Several minutes passed, then Josh heard the sound of a man's voice calling from a little way back from the river. The man seated on the bank responded, and he was shortly joined by another man, who sat down beside him.

Listening to the ensuing conversation, Josh received some very interesting information. The man who had just arrived brought orders from Luke Brent that the men surrounding the homesteads were to leave just before daybreak. They would be replaced by fewer guards whose job was to ensure that nobody left the homesteads during daylight. Later, the night guard would be resumed until after midnight, when a combined assault would be launched on the Foster house by Diamond B hands and Luke Brent's men.

'Mr Brent and Luke have lost patience,' said the man who had just arrived. 'For one thing, it seems Luke has some business to attend to in the Texas Panhandle, and this trouble with the homesteaders is holding him up. When we attack the house, we'll be hitting it from all sides, and the plan is to set fire to the walls so that the settlers will have to come out and give themselves up.'

The conversation which followed was of no interest to Josh, and it was not long before the visitor stood up and left. Then the guard himself rose, and walked away from the bank. Josh waited a few minutes, then continued on his way to the Foster homestead, where his arrival was greeted with considerable relief.

He told Will and the others that the telegraph message would be despatched later in the day. Then he broke the news of the impending night attack on the house.

'We've got to hold out till the law gets here,' said Will, 'and that's going to take more than a day or two. So we've got to beat them off tonight, and make them think again about making another attack on us. We've got supplies to last us over a week, and plenty of weapons and ammunition.'

'How do we deal with them when they come after midnight?' asked Ed.

'I think we should keep the shutters on the four windows closed,' said Will. 'This will stop them from firing through the windows and injuring somebody inside.'

'But how will we fire at them?' asked Josh.

'In each wall of the house,' Will replied, 'we'll cut two holes big enough to poke a rifle or six-gun through, and take aim at anything moving outside. We'll fix something solid on the inside, to cover the holes when they're not in use. So the men moving up to the house will be facing fire from eight weapons. And we'll still have people inside who can do the loading.'

'What about their plan to set fire to the house?' asked Bellamy.

'I'm hoping,' replied Will, 'that with eight people firing at them, they won't have much chance of setting the walls on fire. But, just in case, a little before midnight we'll give the walls a real good soaking with water.'

Will's strategy was agreed, and the holes in the walls were cut during the day. Then the heavy barn doors were securely fastened, to prevent intruders from going inside during the night. At nightfall everyone assembled inside the house for a meal. After this, the young ones were put in an area away from the firing points, and the men and women got the weapons and ammunition ready for use. Firing positions were then allocated to the ones manning the firing points. These would be all six men, plus Jane and Martha. The other three women would help by reloading weapons as required.

When all were clear about their part in the defence of the house, they waited, with some apprehension, for the signals warning of the arrival of the attacking force.

SEVEN

The first alarm wire to be operated was one coming through the front wall of the house. The time was forty minutes after midnight. Quickly, the men and women took up their posts as alarm wires on the other three sides of the house were operated. Outside, the night sky was clear, and it was not long before shadowy figures could be seen stealthily approaching the house on all sides.

As soon as they appeared in view, and before they had time to reach the walls, the attackers, fourteen in all, came under a sudden hail of fire whose intensity was entirely unexpected. Although, in the darkness, accurate shooting was not possible, and not all the defenders were proficient in the use of firearms, four of the attackers were hit, though not fatally, and turned and moved, as quickly as they could, away from the house. A fifth, hit in the leg by a rifle bullet, fell to the ground, then dragged himself painfully away, in the direction from which he had come. All the bullets fired by the attackers embedded themselves harmlessly in the walls of the house.

The attackers, including the two Brents, who had not been hit, realized the danger of continuing their approach on the house, and they hurriedly withdrew. Well back from the house, the rancher and his son stopped to assess the casualties.

Garner, one of Luke Brent's men, had a flesh wound in the left arm. Three Diamond B hands had been hit in the upper body, and one in the leg. None of the wounds appeared to be life-threatening.

'We can't risk another attack now,' said Luke Brent, seething with anger and frustration. 'The wounded men can go back to the ranch. The cook's pretty good at tending gunshot wounds. We've still got enough fit men to keep watch, and make sure nobody leaves the homestead, day or night. We *could* starve them out. They must be running low on supplies by now, and they'll be thinking about the children. But it don't suit me to hang around that long. There must be some quicker way of getting them out of the house. I'll work something out.'

Inside the house, the firing points were manned until daybreak, when it became clear that the Brents had abandoned, for the time being, their plan to storm and take the house.

'There's no doubting,' said Will, 'that we hit several of the men out there, and this probably made them decide not to risk another attack. I'm sure they'll still be watching us, so's they can stop anybody leaving here. We'll carry on watching for anybody heading this way during the day, and during the night we'll stand ready to beat them off again if necessary.'

After breakfast, Will spoke to the homesteaders.

'We've done pretty good so far,' he said, 'but I've been trying to put myself in Luke Brent's place. From what Josh heard on the river bank, Luke's keen to leave here as soon as he can. So maybe he and the others will come back tonight, and try another way of capturing us. I know what *I'd* do if I was in his shoes, and maybe he'll do the same. If he does, we can be ready for him.'

'What d'you have in mind?' asked Josh.

'The walls of the house are pretty thick,' said Will. 'The weakest point is the door. What *I'd* do is take a buckboard, and fix a long stout piece of timber, or maybe a tree trunk, to the bed of the buckboard, with its end sticking out two or three feet at the

95

back. Then I'd pack something on the bed of the buckboard at the back that would catch fire easy, and soak it with lamp oil.

'I'd drive the buckboard here after dark, unhitch the horses, and stand it just out of sight of the guards, with the end pointing straight at the front of the house. As you know, there's a clear flat run right up to the door. Put the right number of men on the tongue, and at the front of the buckboard, who've had practice beforehand in pushing it backward. Then the fire could be lit, and the buckboard pushed backwards until it rammed the house door. The men pushing it would be screened from any gunfire from the house, and the wall would likely catch fire.'

'I can see that Luke Brent might be thinking along those lines,' said Bellamy, 'but what do we do to stop him?'

'There's a simple answer to that,' Will replied, and went on to describe the solution he had in mind.

'It won't take us all that long,' he added, when he had finished. 'Might as well get started on it right now, if you all agree.'

That same morning, on the Diamond B, Luke Brent and his father were discussing their failure to get rid of the homesteaders.

'If it weren't for Drummond,' said Luke, 'I'm sure we'd have driven them out by now. But I reckon there's a way we *can* do it, and I think we should give it a try tonight.'

He went on to describe an operation with a buckboard, which was identical to the one suggested by Will, even down to the burning material which it would carry.

'Let's try it,' said Eli Brent. 'We've got plenty of men for the job. And I'm just as keen as you are to see an end to it.'

During the day, a suitable tree was felled in a nearby grove, The trunk was cut to the required length, which was then trimmed, and fixed firmly to the bed of a buckboard. The end of the trunk was projecting from the rear. The combustible material was then loaded.

A little after midnight, a group of men from the Diamond B rode on to the Foster homestead. One of them was driving the buckboard. They stopped at a point just far enough from the house to ensure that, in the darkness, they could not be seen by the occupants. The riders dismounted, the horses were unhitched, and the buckboard was positioned so that the projecting end of the tree trunk was facing in a direction which led to the door of the house. The two Brents, with the other members of the attacking force, assembled by the tongue and the front of the buckboard, and the combustible material was set on fire. Then, steered by the tongue, the buckboard was pushed backwards, with increasing momentum. Soon the outline of the upper part of the house was visible, and the buckboard was steered towards the centre of the wall, where the door was located. There was no gunfire from the house.

At a point nine yards from the house, when the buckboard was moving at a fair speed, the rear wheels suddenly dropped into a deep wide trench, dug by the homesteaders the previous day, which ran across its path. The buckboard stopped abruptly, and the men who were propelling and steering it, lurched forward and collided with the front. As they recovered their balance, a hail of fire, directed at the buckboard, came from the two holes which had previously been cut in the front wall of the house, and from two additional holes which had been cut in the same wall the day before.

The attackers cowered behind the buckboard, firing an occasional shot towards the house.

Luke Brent cursed. 'We sure can't attack the house from here,' he said. 'We've got to draw back. This buckboard's going to be burnt out before long. We'd better move out while the men firing at us are blinded by the flames.'

They all left the shelter of the buckboard together, and sprinted away from the house. Josh and Will, manning the two holes closest to the side walls, caught a glimpse of them in retreat, and fired a few shots at them before they disappeared into the darkness. Eli Brent was hit in the shoulder, and two Diamond B hands were shot in the arm, though their injuries were not serious. When they reached the horses, Luke Brent helped his father on to his mount.

'We'd better get back to the ranch,' he said. 'We'll have to think up some other way of getting them out.'

They posted guards to keep watch on the homestead, and the rest rode back to the ranch. The cook, who had had some experience in the army as a nursing orderly, looked at the bullet wound in the back of the rancher's shoulder. The bullet was not deeply embedded, and he extracted it without difficulty, and cleaned and dressed the wound. Then he attended to the minor injuries suffered by the two ranch hands. A little later, in the living-room, Luke Brent discussed the problem of the homesteaders with his father.

'I've had an idea,' he said. 'I'm going to send a telegraph message to Armstrong, in Cheyenne. I know he's there. I called to see him on the way up here. He's the man who helped me blow open the safe in a bank in Pueblo. I'll get him to bring some dynamite here, and we'll blast the settlers out of that house. I'll tell him it's urgent. He should be here tomorrow.'

'All right,' said the rancher. 'In the meantime we'd better make sure none of the settlers leaves the homestead.'

When dawn broke on the Foster homestead after the unsuccessful attempt to ram the door of the house, Will and the home-steaders had breakfast. Then, after Will had taken a look at the burnt-out buckboard and the tracks left by the raiders, they assembled to discuss the current situation.

'I know,' said Will, 'that we hit some of them when they were running off. There's some blood on the ground. The question is, what are they going to try next? I've got to say I don't take kindly to just waiting here, wondering what devilry they'll be up to next.'

'I know how you feel,' said Ed, 'but what else can we do?'

'We know,' replied Will, 'that a man on foot can slip by the guards out there, and the Diamond B ranch-house is closer to here than Danford. When they took me there as a prisoner, I noticed there was a big covered water trough just outside the cook-shack. I saw a couple of hands take a drink from it with a ladle, and the cook took some water from it and carried it into the shack. What if I slip out after dark, and put something in that water that don't kill, but puts the men there out of action for a while? We do need a bit more time for the law to get here.'

'Maybe I can help,' said Mary Miller. 'Before Josh and me got married, I worked with a doctor back East for a while, and he invented his own cure for patients with constipation. He taught me how to make it up for him. It didn't have no taste, and you could mix it with water. And it sure did the trick. I never once knew it to fail.'

'That *is* interesting,' said Will. 'Could you make up enough to treat a full trough of water about half as big again as the one outside this house?'

'I reckon I can do that,' said Mary. 'Using what I brought with me, and with the help of the other homesteaders, I should be able to get all the ingredients I need. I'll make up an extra strong mixture that Doc Lilly used to hand out sometimes. He called the remedy Lillylax.'

'A good idea,' said Will. 'It's settled, then. I'll leave after dark, and aim to get there after midnight, when the men who aren't out watching the homestead will likely be asleep. I don't think they'll attack the house tonight, now they know how well it's guarded, and considering their casualties so far, but you'd better keep a watch for them, just the same.'

During the day, Mary, with the help of Jane, prepared sufficient concentrated Lilly-lax to fill a large can.

Will departed with the can, on foot, an hour before midnight, following the same route as that taken by Josh on his recent visit to Danford. When he climbed on to the top of the bank, he headed directly for the Diamond B buildings. So far, he had neither seen nor heard any sign of men from the Diamond B. As he cautiously approached the buildings, it became clear that the Brents had not thought it necessary to station guards.

A light was showing in the bunkhouse, also one in the house. Will walked along the rear of the house, and came up behind the cookshack. He walked along the side, and stopped as he reached the corner. There was no sign of movement outside the buildings. He moved up to the water trough, and lifted the cover. The trough was not quite full of water, and there was plenty of room for the contents of the can, which he poured in. Then he replaced the cover, and left.

On his return journey to the Foster homestead, as he was passing the point where Josh had been delayed by the appearance of one of the guards, he heard the distant sound of voices, which lasted for only a minute or so. He continued on his way to the Foster house, where he gave the pre-arranged signal, and was admitted. He told them his mission had been successful, and they reported that there had been no attack during his absence.

'Good,' said Will. 'Now we just sit tight, and see what Lillylax can do for us.'

EIGHT

On the Diamond B, a little before dawn, the men who were to keep watch on the Foster homestead during daylight had breakfast, and rode out to their posts. The men who had been on night watch returned to the ranch for a meal and some rest.

The first effects resulting from Will's visit during the night were experienced by two hands in the middle of the afternoon, when they were struck down by a succession of severe abdominal pains, interspersed with hurried dashes to the privies. Then, in swift succession, everyone on site, including the two Brents, was affected in a similar way.

The cook, himself suffering badly, was immediately suspected of handing out contaminated food, but he could think of nothing which might have caused the trouble. Water from the trough was not suspected, because it came straight from the river, and the trough was covered, and regularly cleaned out. So, to satisfy the thirst induced by the illness, they all drank water from the trough.

The men watching the Foster homestead, who had taken food and water with them, were also badly affected in the afternoon, but they stuck to their posts, knowing how important it was that no one should be allowed to leave the homestead. At dawn, they were replaced by the day guards, all suffering in the same way as themselves.

Armstrong arrived at the ranch just after noon, carrying the dynamite with him. In the living-room, the Brents told him of the current internal turbulence from which they were all suffering, and which was showing no sign of abating. Then, as they were about to discuss the operation for which Armstrong was being hired, the rancher and his son both rose abruptly and ran out of the room, heading for the privies. They returned ten minutes later.

'We figure it's something we all ate,' said Luke Brent. 'The water we use is all right. Comes straight from the river. Never gave us any trouble. What it was that we ate, we don't know, but *you'll* be all right. The cook will only give you food that can't possibly be contaminated.'

They went on to discuss the operation on the Foster homestead.

'We'll do it tomorrow night,' said Luke

Brent. 'I'm hoping everybody's feeling better by then.'

But early in the evening Armstrong was struck down by exactly the same illness as that affecting the others. Suspicion immediately fell on the water supply, and the trough was drained, thoroughly cleaned, and refilled from the river. From then on, the condition of the affected men started to improve, and on the following morning, at breakfast, it was finally decided that the operation on the Foster homestead would take place during the coming night. Meanwhile, the watch on the homestead would be maintained.

But there was an unexpected development, reported by the men on watch during the night, when they returned shortly after the Brents had finished breakfast. One of their number, a ranch hand called Melville, had disappeared from his post sometime during the night. His horse was still picketed there, but there was no sign of Melville anywhere in the vicinity.

'It's the homesteaders and Drummond,' said Luke Brent. 'Must be. They've snuck out in the night, and captured him. I figure we'll find him there when we raid the place tonight.'

On the afternoon of the day that Armstrong arrived at the Diamond B, a posse of ten men, led by Deputy US Marshal Harding, reached the high ground bordering the south side of the valley. They stopped there and dismounted. US Marshal Harper in Denver, in response to Will's telegraph message, had formed a posse of US deputy marshals, and deputy sheriffs from Colorado and Wyoming, to ride to the aid of the settlers, and arrest Luke Brent's gang of outlaws. In his message, Will had given information on the location of the Foster homestead, and had said that it was under surveillance day and night, by men from the Diamond B.

Harding moved forward to a point from which he had a clear view of the valley below. He soon located the homesteads, and in particular, the Foster homestead. Then he picked out the men who were keeping it under surveillance. He called for one of the deputy sheriffs, a man called Clinton, to join him. Clinton had served as a US Army scout for several years.

Harding handed the glasses to Clinton.

'You can see the Foster homestead, second from the left,' he said, 'and the men watching it. After dark they may move in a bit closer. We need to get through to the

Foster house without Luke Brent knowing about it. So one of the night watchers down there needs to be put out of action, to give us room to slip through in the dark without being noticed.'

'Should be easy,' said Clinton. 'We'll ride into the valley after dark, and I'll go ahead on foot, while the rest of you hang back until I've taken care of the man we need to capture. Then we can all ride on to the house.'

The posse rode down into the valley an hour before midnight. The sky was overcast. Well short of the Foster homestead the posse halted, and Clinton went ahead on foot. Moving soundlessly, and bent almost double, he zigzagged in the general direction of the house, pausing frequently to look and listen. Then he froze as the sudden flare of a match a little way ahead of him, was then partially obscured as Melville, a Diamond B ranch hand standing with his back to the lawman, lit a cigarette.

Clinton dropped down on all fours. Then he crawled silently towards the man ahead until he could see him silhouetted against the night sky, in a standing position, and with his back to the lawman. Clinton rose, and moved noiselessly up to Melville, then pistol-whipped him on the back of his head. Melville collapsed on the ground and before he came to he was gagged and his hands were tied. Then, as soon as he was able to walk, Clinton escorted him back to the other lawmen.

The posse, taking their prisoner with them, rode slowly through the gap and approached the house. They halted well before they could be seen by the people on guard inside, and dismounted.

In his second message to US Marshal Harper, the one which had got through, Will had suggested an exchange of signals which would identify the posse if they approached the house during the night.

Following Will's suggestion, Harding left the others and walked ahead for a short distance. Then he stopped and lit three separate matches at close intervals, allowing each one to burn out. When there was no response after a few minutes, he repeated the process. This time his signal was answered by an identical one given by Will, who had gone outside. Harding called out to the men behind him, and they all moved up to Will, taking the prisoner with them.

Will took them all inside, where they were greeted, with considerable relief by the homesteaders. Harding explained the presence of Melville, who was firmly bound and placed in a small storeroom. Will then gave Harding a concise account of the attempts by the two Brents to get the homesteaders out of the valley.

'I reckon we held them up a bit by doctoring their water supply,' he concluded.

'That accounts,' said Harding, 'for the fact that the prisoner we just brought in was doubled up a couple of times with some sort of belly trouble. We figured it was just fright.'

'That's good to hear,' said Will. 'We're keeping watch, but I don't think they'll attack the house tonight. My guess is that they'll do that about twenty-four hours from now. We know that Luke Brent and his gang are anxious to leave the valley as soon as possible.'

'Right,' said Harding. 'I can see it's a bit crowded in here, but we'd better stay inside with you for the rest of the night. Then, after daybreak, we can arrange a reception for the men from the Diamond B when they turn up.'

'Those alarm wires we rigged up circling the house are still there,' said Will, 'but maybe they're wise to them by now.'

'We can take care of that,' said Harding, and went on to discuss with Will and the homesteaders the strategy for countering the expected assault. Then the posse took some sleep, while the rest maintained their normal night watch for intruders.

The rest of the night was uneventful, and just before dawn Melville was taken to the barn, and left there under guard. The lawmen remained inside during the day, out of sight of any watchers. Immediately after darkness had fallen, Harding sent Clinton out on foot to watch the approaches to the house, so that he could give advance warning of any attack, using the long signal wire which had been installed for Will's use soon after his arrival. This had been checked by Will just before dawn.

'We can count on Clinton,' the posse leader told Will. 'He moves like a shadow in the dark, and his sight and hearing are well above the average.'

All the remaining men started work immediately on the excavation of five short trenches spaced around the house, at points well outside the range of vision from that building after dark. Each trench was just the right size to accommodate two men, and to allow them to fire a rifle over the top. The excavations were completed well before midnight, and timber covers, fashioned during the day, were placed over them. Then they all went into the house, taking the prisoner with them.

In the still night air, just after midnight, Clinton heard the approaching riders when they were still some distance away. He listened to them until he was sure that it was a large group, heading in his direction. He was not far from the end of the alarm wire, and he ran back, grabbed it, and pulled hard. Inside the house a heavy poker, to which the alarm wire was tied, clattered noisily to the floor. It was a signal for the nine lawmen to make an immediate exit with their weapons and run to the five trenches, into one of which Clinton had already dropped. The timber covers were placed nearby so that they could be pulled over at a moment's notice. Inside the house, all the firing points on the walls were manned.

As the lawmen, peering over the tops of the trenches, caught sight of the approaching intruders, all now on foot, they pulled the covers in position. Moments later, the men in three of the trenches heard the sound of footsteps on the cover above. A few minutes later all the covers were cautiously slid aside and the lawmen looked towards the house, on which an attack had not yet been mounted.

Eli Brent, still suffering from his injury, was not a member of the attacking force. Nor were the cook and one other hand. Everybody else was in the party, led by Luke Brent, for this final assault on the house. After dismounting, they formed a circle round the building, and moved forward to positions which were just out of sight of the defenders inside. Luke Brent and Armstrong stood by the side of the barn, which helped to shield them from the house. Armstrong removed from a bag the tied bundle of sticks of dynamite he had brought with him.

'Can you throw it as far as the house from here?' asked Luke Brent.

'Sure,' Armstrong replied. 'It'll drop close to the wall. Should blow a hole right through.'

'Let's get on with it, then,' said the outlaw.

Armstrong lit the fuse cord, which was long enough to ensure that the explosion took place at the right moment. He stepped away from the side of the barn, intending to transfer the bundle from his left to his right hand, ready for the throw.

Standing in a trench some way behind Armstrong and Luke Trent, Harding was looking over the top in their direction. He was holding a rifle in his hands. He saw the flare of the match, followed by the characteristic light given out by a burning fuse cord. Immediately, he realized the intention of the attackers. He aimed his rifle directly at the light, then, as it was blocked by the body of the man holding it, he fired at the point where he guessed the man's upper body would be.

The bullet hit Armstrong in the back. He lurched forward, dropped the bundle of dynamite, and fell down on top of it, with a bullet through his heart. Frantically, Luke Brent dashed round to the back of the barn, barely reaching it before the explosion, which was the signal for the attackers to rush towards the house.

But unaware that the building had not been breached by the explosion, they encountered an unexpected hail of fire from the defenders. Then, on turning back, they found themselves being fired on by the lawmen in their trenches. The only shelter available was the barn, the door of which had not been secured. The men who were still able to, made a dash for this building.

Others, wounded in the leg, hobbled or dragged their way there. Three men, also victims of the gunfire, lay motionless on the ground. When there were no targets left to shoot at, the firing by the defenders ceased.

Inside the barn, there were no openings in the walls, apart from the door. One side wall had been damaged by the blast. The men who had taken refuge there found that five members of the attacking party were missing. These were Armstrong, Luke Brent, Garner, and two Diamond B hands. Of the men inside the barn, five had gunshot wounds in the arm or leg. The whole group was in a desperate situation. They knew that the door of the barn must be well covered by now, and any attempt to escape through it would be suicidal. Then, through a gap in the damaged wall, they heard the voice of Harding calling out to them.

'My name is Deputy US Marshal Harding,' he shouted. 'I'm leading a posse of lawmen. You men are finished. There are thirteen guns trained on the barn. You don't stand a chance. And you've got wounded men in there needing attention. There are four of your partners lying dead out here. As soon as it's light, you'll leave your weapons inside, come out one by one with your arms raised, and stand facing the wall of the barn. And don't figure on trying anything foolish. After that business with the dynamite, we don't much care whether we take you dead or alive.'

Leaving some of the lawmen to keep watch on the barn, Will and Harding went into the house.

'It'll be a while before we know just who's in there,' said Will. 'Maybe we'd better check who's left at the Diamond B. How about me going along there right now with a couple of your men? I know just where the buildings are. I've been there before.'

'All right,' said Harding. 'We'll arrest anybody found there.'

When Will and the two deputy US marshals with him reached the Diamond B ranch-house, there was no sign of anybody outside the buildings, but an oil lamp had been lit in one of the rooms in the house. Will opened the entrance door, and they went in. Light was coming from under a door ahead of them. Cautiously, Will pushed it open and he and his two companions stepped silently into the living-room.

Seated in an armchair by the fire, Eli Brent was dozing, with his chin touching his chest. They moved forward and were almost upon him before he was aware of their presence. His head jerked up and he stared in shocked surprise at Will and the two men wearing deputy US marshal badges.

'Your plan didn't work, Brent,' said Will, 'and four of the men who went to carry it out are dead. The rest have been captured.'

The rancher was visibly shaken. 'Was Luke one of the dead men?' he asked.

'No,' Will replied, 'but there ain't much doubt that he'll hang after he's been before a judge.'

Leaving one deputy with Brent, Will and the other lawman went to the bunkhouse. There they found, in their bunks, the cook and one ranch hand who had been injured during a previous attack on the Foster homestead. Will searched the other buildings without result, after which the two men in the bunkhouse were taken to the house, to be held there with the rancher.

Leaving the two deputies with their prisoners, Will rode back to the Foster homestead and told Harding about the three prisoners who were being held at the ranch. Then, just before dawn, they joined the lawmen outside who were keeping guard on the barn. As the sun rose above the horizon, Harding called out to the men inside.

'Time to come out,' he shouted, and repeated the order twice.

The door started to open, and the deputies raised their weapons. The men inside came out one by one and faced the wall, with hands raised. Several of them were suffering from arm or leg injuries.

The men were searched for weapons, and were then ordered to turn and face their captors. Will had already realized, as the men came out, that Luke Brent was not with them. He checked that there was no one left in the barn, then spoke to Harding.

'I've got bad news,' he said. 'Luke Brent ain't here. I'm sure he'd be leading the attack. He must have slipped away after the explosion.'

'That could be,' said Harding. 'Just before I shot the man holding the dynamite, I thought I saw another man with him. Maybe that was Luke Brent.'

Harding decided to take all the prisoners to the Diamond B, to hold them there pending the arrival of one or more jail wagons to take them to Cheyenne for trial. The injured men would go to the ranch on buckboards, and the doctor in Lantry would be asked to go there to tend to them.

Before the lawmen left with the prisoners

119

Harding spoke to Will.

'We're real obliged for your help,' he said. 'One of Luke Brent's men is dead, and we've got the other two. I guess you're feeling pretty bad about Luke Brent getting away. I heard what he did to your brother. What're you aiming to do now?'

'Get on his trail,' Will replied. 'We know that he and his men had some urgent business in the Texas Panhandle. He's lost his men, but maybe he'll go there anyhow. I'm pretty sure he sent a telegraph message from Lantry a little while back. Ed Foster was captured by the man who took it to the telegraph office for him. I aim to ride there and see if I can find out what was in it. Maybe I'll get some idea of where Luke Brent was figuring to go.'

'I'll go with you,' said Harding. 'Likely I'll get more out of the telegraph operator than you could. And I'll go see the doctor while I'm there. We might as well go right now.'

Leaving the other lawmen to escort the prisoners to the ranch, Will and Harding rode straight to Lantry. First, Harding asked the doctor to go to the Diamond B, then he and Will went to the telegraph office. Harding asked the operator if he remembered anything about the message he had sent just before he was pistol-whipped by Arnold.

'That's a day I ain't going to forget,' he replied. 'I'm still getting a bad headache now and again. As for the message, it was sent to a man called Frost in a little town called Laringo, not far south of Amarillo in the Texas Panhandle. I remember the name Frost because it happens to be my own. The message was signed "Luke". I don't remember exactly what was in it. Something about the sender being held up, but would meet up with him as soon as he could. I don't remember any more than that.'

They thanked Frost and left the office.

'I guess you'll be heading for Laringo?' said Harding.

'That's right,' said Will. 'On the way there I'll call in on the US marshal in Amarillo.'

Will rode back to the valley with Harding, then went on alone to the Foster homestead. By the time he arrived there, all the other homesteaders had returned to their own quarter sections, and were busy tending their crops. Will told the Fosters about the information given him by the telegraph operator.

'I'll leave for the Texas Panhandle in the morning,' he said. 'I have a strong hunch that's where Luke Brent is heading.'

'We're real obliged to you for the way you helped us,' said Ed. 'Now we can carry on running our homesteads without having to worry all the time about what the Brents were aiming to do to us next.'

NINE

Will rode to the nearest home station on a stagecoach route in Wyoming, then travelled by stage to Amarillo. When he finally arrived there it was late in the evening. The following morning he went to see US Marshal Edison. The marshal was a tall lean man, with a neat black moustache and a keen eye. He listened to Will's story with interest.

'That's good news about Luke Brent losing all his men,' he said. 'The gang's caused us a heap of trouble here in the Panhandle and further south. So you reckon Luke Brent might be heading for Laringo?'

'I think there's a good chance of that,' said Will. 'I'm going to get me a horse and ride down there. I don't suppose you've heard of a man called Frost living in that area?'

'No, I haven't,' Edison replied. 'But I'd sure like to get my hands on Luke Brent. If you do locate him, get word to me and I'll send you help.'

Will left Amarillo shortly after, riding south. He had reached a point which he guessed was about eight miles short of his destination, when he saw a homestead on his left. He rode towards the house, intending to ask for water for his horse, and to check whether he was on the right course for Laringo. As he neared the house, he saw a buggy standing outside it, with a horse hitched to it. Two other horses, both saddled, were tied to a hitching-rail, and as one of them moved, Will could see that it was lame.

An hour prior to the arrival of Will at the Sinclair homestead, Anne Kincaid had arrived in the buggy. Her brother Andrew was a doctor living in Laringo, and Anne spent a lot of her time helping him in his work. She was a slim attractive woman, auburn-haired, and in her late twenties. She had plenty of male admirers in Laringo and the surrounding area, but as far as she was concerned, the right man had not yet come along.

She had driven out to the homestead with some medicine for Sinclair, who had been struck down with a fever the previous day, when her brother had visited him, but had been unable to diagnose the cause. Mrs Sinclair took Anne into the bedroom, where her husband was lying on the bed.

'He's got worse since yesterday,' she said. 'His temperature's real high, and he starts rambling every now and then. Don't know where he is.'

Anne took the patient's temperature. It was dangerously high.

'I'm going back to town,' she said. 'I'll get Andrew to come out here right away. Maybe, this time, he'll be able to tell what's causing the trouble.'

There was a knock on the door of the house, and Mrs Sinclair walked to the bedroom window and looked out. Two men, both strangers to her, were standing outside. She went to the door and opened it. She felt a vague sense of unease as she looked at the two armed men, one tall and heavily built, the other short, but almost as broad as his partner.

'Howdy,' said the big stranger. 'Your man around?'

'He's took sick,' said Mrs Sinclair. 'He's in bed. What did you want with him?'

The men did not reply. They pushed the woman back into the house, then bundled her into the bedroom. Each of them was holding a six-gun in his right hand. Alarmed, Anne, who had been sitting by the bed, rose to her feet as they came into the room.

'Who's this?' asked the big man, looking at Anne.

'She's just brought some medicine from the doctor in Laringo,' the homesteader's wife replied. 'What d'you want from us?'

'We ain't eaten for quite a spell,' he replied, 'so you can whip up a meal for us. And when we leave, we'll be taking one of your horses with us, on account of one of ours is lame. You can get started on that meal right now. And don't do anything foolish or I'll have to beat up this man of yours.'

Sinclair's wife went into the kitchen, followed by the short man, and hastily prepared a meal. The big man stayed in the bedroom, guarding Anne and Sinclair. Leering at Anne, he tried, unsuccessfully, to draw her into conversation. When the meal was ready it was brought into the bedroom and there the two men wolfed it down. During the meal, much to Anne's discomfort, the big man's gaze settled on her from time to time. When the meal was over he spoke to her.

'Just one thing to do now before we leave,' he said. 'It's quite a while since I had any female company. I reckon we should get better acquainted. We'll go over to the barn. It's more private there.'

He moved towards Anne, who was preparing to resist him as best she could. Then he halted as through the partly open window he caught sight of Will riding up to the house. He also saw that Will was armed.

'Watch these three,' he said to his partner. 'We've got company. If either of these women tries to raise the alarm, shoot her.'

He holstered his gun and went outside. Will, who had just dismounted, stood facing him. Will knew immediately that this armed man was not a homesteader. In fact, based on his previous experience, he thought it very likely that he was looking at a criminal. He wondered what the man was doing here, and where was the man who had been riding the second horse at the hitching-rail? He sensed the danger in the air.

'I'd be obliged for some water for my horse,' he said, 'and for directions to Laringo.'

The big man pointed to a nearby water trough. 'Help yourself,' he said, 'and Laringo's about eight miles due south of here.'

He watched Will closely as he watered his horse.

In the bedroom, Sinclair, who had been lying unconscious since the arrival of the two strangers, opened his eyes. He saw a man pointing a gun at his wife and Anne. The man's back was partly turned towards him, and he sat up and made a grab for the gun. But he was too weak to succeed, and the stranger turned and pistol-whipped him on the head. He fell back on the bed, and lay there, motionless. His wife screamed and ran towards him, but pulled up short as the stranger's gun was jammed into her body. Anne stayed still, fearing that any move on her part would cause the man to trigger his gun.

As Will finished watering his horse, he heard the shrill scream through the partly open window of the bedroom. He was facing Lloyd, the man standing near the door watching him.

'Somebody in trouble in there?' he asked.

'None of your business,' said Lloyd. 'You'd best be moving on.'

'Not just yet,' said Will. 'I aim to take a look inside.'

The man facing Will went for his gun, but Will was ready for him. His draw was just a shade faster than that of his opponent, who collapsed on the ground with a bullet through the heart. Quickly, Will checked that the man lying on the ground was dead.

Then he went up to the door, where he was out of sight of anybody who might be standing at the bedroom window. He guessed that the man he had just shot had a partner who was in the bedroom.

He entered the house and approached the bedroom door, which was slightly ajar. He paused as he heard, coming from inside the room, the voice of Randle, partner of the dead man lying outside. Randle had heard the gunshot.

'You all right, Jed?' he shouted.

'Jed ain't in no fit state to answer,' Will shouted back. 'He pulled a gun on me, but he weren't fast enough. You'd best throw your gun down and come out with your hands up.'

Inside the bedroom Randle, who was standing close to Anne, with his six-gun in his hand, suddenly moved up to her, clamped his arm around her neck, and held the end of the barrel of his gun against the side of her head. The hammer was cocked. Anne realized the danger of struggling, and forced herself to stay calm.

'I'm holding a woman in here, with a gun against her head,' shouted Randle, 'and the hammer's cocked. We're coming out now. But first I want you to drop your gun just inside this room.'

Will ran softly to Lloyd's body and picked up the gun lying on the ground nearby. He tucked this gun out of sight underneath the back of his belt, where it was concealed by his vest. Then he ran softly back to the door of the bedroom, and dropped his own weapon just inside.

A moment later, Randle pulled the door open with his foot and ordered Mrs Sinclair to walk out, in front of him and Anne. He told Will and the homesteader's wife to go outside, then followed them, still holding his prisoner. He saw his partner's body lying on the ground.

'We're going for a ride in the buggy,' he said to Anne, releasing his hold on her, 'and if anybody follows us, you'll be shot. Climb on the buggy now. You'll be doing the driving.'

With Will and Mrs Sinclair watching, and Randle pointing the gun at her head, Anne put her right foot on the step, then her left foot on to the floor of the buggy. She raised her right foot to follow the left, then suddenly kicked backwards with all her strength, then immediately dropped on to the floor of the buggy, in front of the seat. The blow in the groin from the heel of

Anne's boot raised a howl of pain from Randle which coincided with the firing of his gun. The bullet passed harmlessly through the space occupied by Anne's head a moment before. Still holding his gun, and with his eyes watering profusely, Randle dropped to his knees on the ground. Startled by the gunshot, the horse which was hitched to the buggy took off, and the buggy moved rapidly away from the house.

Will reached behind his back for the gun tucked under his belt, and tried to slide it out. But the front sight on top of the barrel caught on his belt, and by the time he had freed it, Randle had stood up and turned to face him. The two men fired at the same time. A bullet plucked the side of Will's vest, before passing harmlessly on. His opponent staggered back as a bullet drilled into his chest. Then he collapsed on the ground, dropping his gun.

Will ran up to him and picked up the weapon. Then he looked to see how far the buggy had gone. Relieved, he saw that it had turned, and was now heading for the house. Anne was obviously in control. As he bent down to look at the man he had just shot, Randle drew his last breath. Will straightened up and awaited the arrival of the buggy, while Mrs Sinclair rushed in to tend to her husband.

As Anne drew near to the house, she saw Will waiting for her. Behind him, lying on the ground, were the two men who had held her and the Sinclairs prisoner. She brought the buggy to a stop, and Will helped her out.

'Those two lying there ain't going to trouble nobody no more,' he said. 'And you had a big hand in that. I sure admire the way you got the better of the man who was aiming to ride off with you. That took some grit.'

'I wasn't thinking clear at the time,' said Anne, still somewhat unnerved by recent happenings. 'Just didn't fancy the idea of taking a ride with a man like that. We sure were lucky you happened along. I'm Anne Kincaid. My brother Andrew is the doctor in Laringo.'

'Will Drummond,' said Will. 'just passing by, on the way to Laringo.'

'I must see to Mr Sinclair,' she said. 'He's in bed with a fever. And one of those two hit him on the head.'

She ran into the house. Will followed her into the bedroom. The homesteader, his wife by his side, was still unconscious, with an angry bruise showing on his head.

'I need to get my brother here as soon as I can,' said Anne, 'but I think I should stay with the patient till he gets here.'

'I'll drag those two bodies in the barn,' said Will, 'then I'll ride to Laringo as fast as I can. What do I tell your brother?'

'Say Mr Sinclair's got a very high temperature, with unconscious spells,' said Anne, 'and on top of that he's been pistol-whipped on the head.'

When Will reached Laringo, he soon located the doctor's house near the middle of town. It was a well-built painted timber structure, with a neat fenced-in garden at the front. He found the doctor inside, and quickly explained the situation to him.

'I'll leave now,' said Kincaid. 'I'll pick up a horse at the livery stable. The liveryman will arrange for those two bodies to be picked up. D'you reckon they were outlaws?'

'I think it's very likely,' Will replied.

'We owe you a lot,' said Kincaid. 'If you're aiming to stay here for a while, Anne and I will see you when we get back. Meantime, come with me to the livery stable. I'd like you to meet the liveryman, Ike Mason. He's a good friend of mine. You can tell him yourself what happened at the homestead.'

They went to the stable, where the doctor quickly introduced Will to Mason, then made a hurried departure. Will recounted the recent events at the homestead, and asked if the two bodies could be collected from the barn.

'The blacksmith next door does all the undertaking around here,' said Mason. 'I'll go see him right away.'

'I'll hang around here till you get back,' said Will. 'There's some information you might be able to give me.'

When Mason returned, Will asked him if he knew anybody called Frost in or around Laringo.

'I only know one man of that name,' the liveryman replied. 'That's Frost the telegraph operator. He also acts as an agent for Wells Fargo. You can see the telegraph office across the street. He lives in the little house next door.'

'What sort of a man is he?' asked Will.

'He's single,' Mason replied, 'and he spends a lot of time in the saloon. Likes a game of cards, and sometimes loses heavily, so they say. Takes a long ride out of town now and then. Don't know where he goes. He's been here about a year. I'd say he was in his middle-thirties.'

'That's very interesting,' said Will, then went on to give a detailed description of the two dead men, on whom he had found no indication of their identities.

'D'you know those two?' he asked.

Mason said that they were strangers to him. Will asked him not to mention to anyone that he had been asking questions about Frost. Then he went to the hotel, which was close by, on the same side of the street. He took a room which overlooked the street and gave a clear view of the telegraph office and adjoining house. He sat down by the window, and considered the situation.

It seemed almost certain that Luke Brent's telegraph message had been intended for Frost, the telegraph operator, who had passed on to a criminal acquaintance of Brent's the information that it contained. And this criminal was probably hiding out not far from Laringo. And was the fact that Frost was a Wells Fargo agent significant? Was he passing on information about valuable Wells Fargo shipments?

It was now dark outside, and Will went to the hotel dining-room for a meal. When he had finished, he went upstairs to his room. At around the same time Frost walked into the saloon, where the talk was about the events at the Sinclair homestead earlier that day. He listened as a townsman who had been talking to the liveryman described the events, mentioning that the two dead men were strangers, one tall and heavily-built, the other much shorter. He added that the blacksmith had gone to pick up the bodies.

The brief description of the two dead men caught Frost's attention. He himself was being paid by the leader of a gang of outlaws for information about Wells Fargo shipments, and for other services. He knew that two members of the gang, Lloyd and Randle, were due to rejoin Curtis, the leader, at his hide-out, after a brief absence. Frost had once met the two men at the hide-out, and they tallied with the rough description he had just heard. He decided that he had to find out if Lloyd and Randle were, in fact, dead, so that he could let Curtis know.

He went back to his house, and kept watch on the blacksmith's shop for the return of the buckboard carrying the two bodies. It arrived an hour before midnight. The two men on the driver's seat climbed down and carried the two bodies inside. One of them came out shortly after, but it was an hour before Frost saw the blacksmith himself leave and go to his house.

Frost waited another half-hour, then slipped out of his house on to the deserted street. He entered the blacksmith's shop, which was not normally secured, and found the two bodies lying on the floor, under a canvas sheet. He pulled the sheet back to reveal the heads, then struck a match. Immediately, he could see that the bodies were those of Lloyd and Randle. He pulled the sheet back in position and returned, unobserved, to his house. He decided that he would take some time off the following day in order to ride to advise Curtis of the loss of two of his men. And before he left, he would find out more about the man who had killed them.

TEN

When Frost woke on the morning after his identification of the two bodies, he had breakfast. Then he walked along to see Daley, the blacksmith. He had heard the previous evening that the man who had killed Lloyd and Randle was called Drummond. He told Daley that he had been friendly with a man of that name when he was working in Amarillo, and he asked the blacksmith to describe him.

'No need for that,' said Daley. 'See for yourself. He's over there, coming out of the hotel with the doctor.'

Frost looked closely at Will as he walked along the street, then into the doctor's house. Then he turned to Daley.

'That's not my friend,' he said. 'He's not like him at all. Is he staying on in town?'

'For a short while, as far as I know,' Daley replied.

Inside the doctor's house, to which Will had been invited by Kincaid, Will sat down with Andrew and Anne. They both thanked him for his intervention at the homestead the previous day, then told him that Sinclair's fever had broken the previous evening, and despite the knock on the head, he was recovering well.

'Are you staying in town for a while, Mr Drummond?' asked Anne who, despite their short acquaintance, felt strongly attracted to the stranger.

'For a few days at least,' replied Will, thinking that this was a woman he would like to have the chance of knowing much better. He decided to tell her and her brother of the reason for his presence in the area, starting with the death of his brother.

'I'm pretty sure,' he went on, 'that Frost is in cahoots with criminals hiding somewhere around here, and I think it's likely that Luke Brent is either with them now, or will be soon. The next time Frost rides out of town, I aim to follow him.'

'Frost keeps his horse at the livery stable,' said the doctor. 'If you tell your story to Ike Mason, the livery-man, I can guarantee that like us, he'll keep it to himself. And he'd let you know immediately Frost leaves town on one of his rides. Shall I bring him here?'

Will agreed, and so it was arranged with Mason.

Will left soon after, and when he had gone Kincaid looked closely at his sister.

'I know you pretty well, Anne,' he said, 'and I reckon you've taken a shine to Drummond. Am I right?'

'You don't miss much, do you?' Anne said, smiling. 'He's different from the men I meet around here. He carries a gun and obviously knows how to use it. But he uses it to uphold the law. I think he's a good man.'

'I feel the same way myself,' said the doctor. 'It's a dangerous job he's taken on. Let's hope he manages to pull it off.'

Rather sooner than expected, the liveryman brought the news to Will at the hotel, half an hour after noon, that Frost had just ridden off.

'He's heading east,' said Mason. 'Your horse is saddled and ready to go.'

Will went back with him to the stable, taking a pair of high-powered field-glasses with him. He rode to the edge of town, then stopped and watched the distant rider until he disappeared from view over the top of a distant rise. He waited for a short while, then rode fast to the rise, dismounted near the top, and crawled forward until he could see the ground on the far side.

He was just in time to see Frost riding

through a gap in a low ridge ahead. He continued to shadow him, noticing that the man ahead of him appeared to have no suspicion that he might be followed. They had travelled about fourteen miles in an easterly direction, and were in an area of rough ground, far from any recognized trails, when Will, watching from cover, saw Frost ride up to the entrance to a narrow ravine, and stop. As he did so, a man appeared from behind a large boulder standing at the top of the wall of the ravine. A moment later, he appeared to wave the rider on, and Frost disappeared from view, while the man retreated behind the boulder.

Will stayed where he was, confident that he had located the hide-out of the gang which Luke Brent had intended to join, and aware that he could not continue any further, in daylight, without being spotted.

Waved on by Jackson, one of the Curtis gang, Frost rode on up the ravine, towards an old, long-abandoned shack. Two men were seated on the ground outside. They were Curtis, and Lester, a member of his gang. Curtis, a slim man of average height, had a long cruel face, and there was a menacing look about him. Frost rode up, dismounted, and joined the two men.

'It's bad news,' he said, and went on to tell the outlaw leader about the deaths of two of his men, Lloyd and Randle.

'Damnation!' said Curtis. 'Just when we were getting ready for a big operation. They were both fools. I told them not to get into any trouble while they were away. This man Drummond. What's he like?'

Frost gave him a fairly accurate description of Will, then changed the subject.

'Looks like Brent ain't turned up yet,' he said.

'That's right,' said Curtis. 'I'm counting on him getting here soon. We need him and his men more than ever now. Have you got any more news about that big gold shipment?'

'Not yet,' Frost replied. 'I think it might be passing through around a couple of weeks from now. As soon as I have anything definite, I'll let you know. I'd best be getting back now.'

Will saw Frost leave the ravine and head back towards him. He hid with his horse in a small nearby gully until Frost had passed. Then he returned to his previous position, and through his field-glasses, he carefully surveyed the area around the hide-out. He was looking for a place where he could hide and keep the inside of the ravine under fairly close observation. The most promising place was a large patch of brush located at the top of the wall of the ravine, well away from the look-out's position.

An hour later, it was dark enough for Will to start riding towards the hide-out. Keeping well away from the look-out post, he located the patch of brush. It was tall and thick enough for his purpose, and from it he could see the faint light showing through a window of the shack.

He looked round for a place where he could hide his horse, and found a small gully nearby which was suitable. He had a meal there, using provisions he had brought with him. Then he rested until half an hour before dawn, when he walked with his field-glasses to the brush patch, leaving his picketed horse behind him. He chose a place in the brush from which he had a clear view of the shack and the lookout point.

When the light improved sufficiently he could see the look-out standing against the boulder. At eight o'clock a man appeared in view and walked over to relieve the look-out, who went into the shack. Through his glasses, Will was able to see that neither of these men was Luke Brent. A little later, a third man came out briefly to pick up some pieces of timber. But once again, it was not Brent. During the rest of the day the two men first spotted by Will, continued to act as look-out, relieving each other at four-hour intervals. Will guessed that the third man, who appeared outside the shack now and then, was the leader of the gang. And unless Brent was, for some reason, not leaving the shack, it appeared that he was not at the hide-out. When darkness fell, Will returned to his horse, and took some supper. He had decided to continue watching the hide-out during the daytime, in the hope that Luke Brent would turn up shortly.

He kept watch for the next three days, during which he saw no sign of Luke Brent. By then he had run out of provisions, and as he walked back to his horse in the darkness, he decided to ride to Laringo for supplies, then return before daybreak to resume his watch.

The sky was overcast as he walked into the gully and up to his horse, speaking softly to it as he approached. As he walked behind the animal, he felt a sudden premonition of danger. But it came too late. Pistol-whipped on the head by the man hiding on the other side of his mount, he fell to the ground. When he came to a few minutes later, his hands were tightly bound, and his six-gun had been taken from its holster. Shakily, he rose to his feet.

'I'm taking a ride, and you're taking a walk behind me,' said Tobin, the man in front of him. 'Try anything foolish, and I'll gun you down.'

Tobin was a member of the Curtis gang on his way to rejoin the others at the hide-out, after a brief visit to relatives in South Texas. He held the free end of the length of rope binding Will's hands, and walked out of the gully, leading Will and his horse. When he reached the place where he had hidden his own mount, he climbed into the saddle, tied the rope he was holding to the pommel, and led Will and his horse towards the position of the look-out.

When he was within hailing distance, Tobin called out to identify himself, saying he had a prisoner with him. Lester, standing near the boulder, told him to go on in. When they arrived at the shack, Curtis and Jackson were inside, taking supper. Tobin picketed the two horses, keeping a close watch on Will. Then he led the prisoner to the door of the shack, and called out to identify himself before opening the door and pushing Will inside in front of him. Seated at a rickety table, Curtis and Jackson stared in surprise at Tobin's prisoner.

'Look what I found,' said Tobin, 'in a gully close to here. When I was riding in just before dark I spotted a horse in the gully, but no sign of the owner. So I waited for him to turn up. I figure maybe he's been spying on you. D'you know him?'

The two men seated at the table both shook their heads.

'He's a stranger to me,' said Curtis, but then realized that the prisoner could be, from Frost's description, the man called Drummond who had killed Lloyd and Randle at the homestead. But even if he were that man, how did he come to be here, and why would he be spying on the hide-out?

He took Tobin outside, and told him about the deaths of Lloyd and Randle. He said there was a possibility that the prisoner might be the man who had killed them. They went back inside, and Curtis spoke to Will.

'You like to tell us just what you're doing here?' he asked.

'Just happened by,' said Will. 'I'm heading

for Fort Worth. Was figuring to camp out in the gully for the night. Went out to look for some firewood, but there weren't none to be found nearby. My name's Carson.'

Curtis told Tobin to search Will, but this produced no evidence as to his identity.

'I think you're lying,' said Curtis, 'and there's one way I can find out for sure. Meanwhile you'll be staying here.'

He took Jackson outside, and told him that the prisoner might be the killer of Lloyd and Randle. He told him to ride to Laringo and ask Frost to come out as soon as he could, in order to tell them whether the prisoner was Drummond or not.

When Jackson reached Laringo he went into Frost's office, and gave him the message.

'It could be him,' said Frost. 'I ain't seen him around since yesterday. I'm busy just now, but I should be able to ride out late in the afternoon.'

As Jackson was leaving the telegraph office, Anne Kincaid was walking along the other side of the street. Jackson was a stranger to her, and she wondered, idly, what he was doing in town. She saw him mount his horse and ride off to the east.

When Frost reached the hide-out later, night was falling. The look-out told him to knock at the cabin door, then wait outside. When he had done this, Curtis came out, and stayed with Frost while Will was blindfolded. Then the two men went inside, and Frost looked at Will. He nodded his head and went outside again with Curtis.

'That's Drummond all right,' he said. 'What in blazes brought him here?'

'That's what I'm wondering,' said Curtis. 'We've got–' He broke off as he heard the distant sound of voices coming from the direction of the look-out position. 'Sounds like we have a visitor,' he said.

They waited, and it was not long before they saw a rider approaching them. As he stopped and dismounted, both men recognised Luke Brent.

'We'd near given you up,' said Curtis. 'And I didn't figure you'd turn up on your own. Where are those three men of yours?'

Quickly, Brent told Curtis of the intention of himself and his father to force the homesteaders out of the valley where the Diamond B was located. Then he went on to describe the complete and disastrous failure of their plan, and the consequent loss of all three of his men.

'We've had a bit of a setback ourselves,' said Curtis. 'Randle and Lloyd were killed not far from here, on their way back to the hide-out. They called at a homestead, aiming to steal a horse, but a stranger called Drummond, who happened to call there at the time, gunned them both down.'

'That's quite a coincidence,' said Brent. 'The man who organized the homesteaders to beat us in Wyoming was called Drummond as well. It seems he was just a drifter who happened along and sided with them.'

'Well,' said Curtis, 'it so happens we've got the Drummond who killed Lloyd and Randle tied up inside the shack. Frost just identified him. He's blindfolded. Didn't want him to know Frost was helping us.'

'I'd best be leaving,' said the telegraph operator. 'I've heard nothing about that gold shipment yet. Are you still interested?'

'Right now, we ain't got enough men to do the job,' said Curtis, 'but I think I know where I can get some more to make up the numbers. So let us know when you have any definite information.'

Frost rode off, and the two outlaws entered the shack, with Curtis in the lead. When Brent saw the blindfolded prisoner, his chin dropped and his eyebrows shot up. He grabbed the arm of Curtis, and led him outside.

'Well I'm damned!' he said. 'That's the same Drummond we were up against in Wyoming. I just can't figure out how he comes to be down here. Has he talked yet?'

'Before Frost identified him,' Curtis replied, 'he said his name was Carson, and that he was on his way to Fort Worth when we picked him up.'

'We've got to find out why he turned up here,' said Brent. 'Is he after me, and if so, why? And does anybody else know about the hide-out? We've got to get the truth out of him before we kill him, and I guess it ain't going to be easy.'

The two men went inside, and the blind-fold was taken off the prisoner. Seeing Brent, Will knew that his hunch had been correct. Brent spoke to him.

'What we want to know, Drummond,' he said, 'is your reason for being here, and how it was you managed to find this hide-out. Whatever it takes, we'll get the truth out of you, but maybe you'd like to do it the easy way, and tell us right now.'

Hoping that a chance to escape might turn up, and knowing that he was due to die whether he told the truth or not, Will decided to stick to his previous story, while admitting giving a false name.

'After we'd put things right in Wyoming,' he said, 'I headed out to visit kinfolk at Fort Worth. I didn't have no choice about shooting down the two men at the homestead, and when I was picked up here, I used the name Carson in case the two men had been heading for this place.'

'Not good enough,' said Brent. 'We'll have to get the truth out of you the hard way.'

He turned to Curtis. 'Is there an axe and a shovel around?' he asked.

'Sure,' replied Curtis, 'standing in the corner there.'

'Good,' said Brent. 'What we'll do tomorrow then, is visit that grove I passed a little while back, and cut the timber for three poles. Then we'll plant two of them outside the shack and fasten the third across the tops. We'll bind Drummond's hands and feet, and tie his hands to the cross-pole. We'll leave him hanging there at full stretch, without food and water. It's something I've tried before. It shouldn't be all that long before we get the truth out of him.'

Will, bound hand a foot, spent the night lying on the floor of the shack. In the morning, Brent and Jackson rode out to the grove, and brought back the roughly-fashioned poles. They set two of them firmly in the ground, four feet apart, and fastened the third to the tops of the others. Then they brought Will out of the shack and tied him to the horizontal pole so that he was hanging fully stretched, with his feet six inches above the ground.

'Just sing out when you feel like telling the truth, Drummond,' said Brent, before disappearing into the shack with Jackson.

Will, his body gently swaying and turning in the breeze, could see no possibility of escape, unaided, while he was suspended this way. The strain on his arms was beginning to tell, and he knew that no food or drink would be given to him. The outlook was not good.

Returning from a visit to one of her brother's patients out of town, two days after Will had been captured, Anne Kincaid drove a buggy up to the livery stable in Laringo, where the horse and buggy were kept. As she stepped down from the buggy, Mason, the liveryman, came out to greet her. At the same time, a stranger who had just ridden into town stopped close by. He was a cheerful-looking man in his thirties, average in size, wearing a Montana peak hat. He smiled amiably at Anne and Mason.

'Howdy, folks,' he said, tipping the brim of

his hat to Anne. 'I'm looking for a friend of mine called Will Drummond. Heard he might be here. Happen you've met him?'

Mason looked at Anne, then spoke to the stranger. 'You know him pretty well?' he asked.

'We go back a long way,' the stranger replied. 'I'm Roy Dillon. Will and his brother Clint and myself all worked together as lawmen for a spell in Kansas. The three of us were pretty close. Then I moved to Amarillo a few years back and started running a general store. It's doing pretty well. A few days ago, a friend of mine in the Texas Rangers told me that Clint had been killed by Luke Brent, and that Will had come down here looking for the killer. I left a friend running the store, and rode here to see if I could help.'

'We're sure glad to see you,' said Anne. 'My name's Anne Kincaid. Will Drummond saved me when I was in real trouble, and now he's gone missing. We're worried about what might have happened to him.'

She and Mason then gave Roy an account of events since Will's arrival in the area.

'When he left town to follow Frost,' said Anne, 'he didn't have enough provisions to last until now, and he told us he'd come

154

back here whether or not he found what he was looking for. So I'm worried something's happened to him. I was going to speak to my brother and ask if he could get one or two men from town to join him in a search for Mr Drummond.'

'He can count me in, Anne,' said the liveryman.

'Better to leave it to me,' said Roy. 'I reckon a man riding alone would stand a better chance of finding Will. Have you any idea at all where Frost was going when Will followed him?'

'He was heading east,' said Mason, 'and judging by the length of time he was away, and allowing for him staying with the gang for about thirty minutes, I'd say the hide-out was between thirteen and fifteen miles from here, to the east. That's if he didn't change direction after he'd left here.'

'Well, that's something to go on,' said Roy. 'I'll have a meal, get me some provisions, then I'll ride off to the east and see what turns up.'

Anne and Mason wished Roy success in his search. He had a meal, then bought some provisions at the general store. As he was leaving it, Mason hurried up to him.

'You're in luck,' he said. 'Frost just picked

up his horse.' He pointed along the street. 'You can see him leaving town, heading east. There's a chance he's going to the hide-out.'

Roy thanked Mason, the liveryman, and followed Frost, employing exactly the same tactics which Will had used. Eventually, from cover, and using field-glasses, he watched Frost speak to the look-out and enter the ravine.

When Frost reached the hide-out shack, he told Curtis and Brent that he had firm information that a Wells Fargo express wagon, with armed guards on board, would be passing through Amarillo in a southerly direction in six days' time. It would be carrying a gold shipment of considerable value. He gave details of the route to be followed by the wagon.

When Frost left, the two outlaws discussed the possibility of robbing the wagon.

'We're a bit short on men now,' said Curtis, 'and we ain't got the time to get hold of any more. But I reckon it's too good a chance to turn down. What d'you think?'

'I know one man I might be able to get quick,' said Brent, 'and a good man at that. He's a cousin of mine. He's called Wilson. Spends most of his time playing crooked poker, but he's helped me out now and then. If I can get him I reckon we can safely rob the express wagon. I'm pretty sure that right now he's in a town only twenty-five miles south of here. If I start off right now, we'll be back here tomorrow.'

Curtis agreed with Brent's suggestion, so Brent left shortly after Frost's departure but by a different route, so was not seen by Roy.

Roy continued watching from cover until Frost reappeared twenty minutes later, and rode past him on his way to Laringo in the gathering darkness. Then Roy rode on towards the ravine and found a place close to the patch of brush from which Will had kept watch on the hide-out in the ravine below. He could see that a lamp was burning inside the shack. Continuing to watch, he settled down to wait for a few hours. Around midnight, he saw the shack door open and a man come out, closing the door behind him. Ten minutes later a man opened the door of the shack and went inside. Roy guessed that the look-out had just been relieved.

He waited a further half-hour, then made his way slowly down the sloping side of the ravine to the bottom. The shack was now between him and the look-out position. Cautiously, he moved forward, passing a picket line with five horses tied to it. As he drew near to the shack, he saw the dim outlines of two posts standing a little way from the side of it, with something swinging in between them. He paused for a few minutes, then moved up to the posts. He could now see that a man was suspended from a cross-pole above. He was sure he had found his friend. This was confirmed when he walked up close, looked up at the prisoner's face, and spoke softly to him.

'Will,' he said. 'This is Roy.'

Will, hanging in extreme discomfort, with his eyes closed, thought for a moment that he was dreaming. Then he heard the words repeated. He opened his eyes and saw Roy in front of him.

'Roy,' he said faintly. 'Am I glad to see you. There are three men in the shack and one look-out.'

'Let me get you down,' said Roy, and looked round for something which would raise him high enough to be able to cut the rope just above Will's hands. He soon found a short section of tree trunk which had been used as a chopping block. He placed it in position and stood on it, then reached up with his knife to sever the rope. Will, suddenly realizing what was happening, shook his head, and spoke to him urgently

'No!' he said. 'There's an alarm cord tied round my neck. It goes through a staple on top of the pole, then into the hut. I watched Luke Brent rigging it up. I reckon that any pull on it would raise the alarm. Before you cut me down you'll have to cut the cord and tie it fast somewhere, without pulling on it.'

Roy felt for the cord, cut it with care, and tied it off around the staple. Then he cut the rope holding Will to the cross-pole, and lowered him to the ground. Quickly, he cut the ropes binding Will's hands and feet, then asked his friend how he was feeling.

'Mighty thirsty,' Will replied, 'and my arms feel like they don't belong to me. Let's walk up the ravine out of sight of the shack. Then I'll get my arm working again, and we'll decide what to do next. I don't think anybody's going to notice I'm missing until the look-out's relieved at four o'clock.'

They walked up the ravine for a short distance, then Will sat down while Roy went up to his horse and brought back his water canteen and some food for Will. He also handed him a loaded six-gun and some spare cartridges. Will tucked the gun under his belt, and pocketed the cartridges. Then he ate and drank the food and water. While doing this he told Roy what had happened since he had followed Frost to the hide-out.

'So Luke Brent's in the shack, then?' said Roy.

'I was coming to that,' said Will. 'He ain't here. He rode off right after Frost left yesterday. Before he left I overheard some of them talking. I got the idea that Brent was riding somewhere to find a few men willing to join the gang. I don't know when he'll be back. But how come *you're* here yourself, Roy?'

'Heard in Amarillo,' said Roy, 'that you were chasing Clint's killer. Figured you might need a hand.'

'Looks like you were right,' said Will. 'Now we've got to figure out how to capture the three men in the shack, and the look-out.'

After a brief discussion, they walked back to the picket line, collected a coil of rope lying on the ground, then advanced on the shack. Quietly, Will opened the door and stepped inside, with Roy close behind him. Each of them was holding a six-gun in his hand. A lighted oil lamp, with the wick turned well down, was standing on a table. Three men, all asleep, were lying on bedrolls on the floor.

Will turned up the lamp, and Roy quickly

removed the six-guns lying close to the three sleeping men. Then he joined Will and they both stood looking down at the men lying on the floor.

Curtis was the first one to become aware of their presence. Disturbed by the increase in lighting, he stirred, and his eyes opened. He stared up at the two men looking down on him, and his hand reached out instinctively for his gun. But it was not there.

'Just stay exactly where you are, Curtis,' said Will, 'or I'll shoot you.'

The sound of his voice woke the other two men, and they also were ordered to stay down. Then all three were told to lie face down. While Will held a gun on them, Roy gagged them, and bound their hands and feet with the rope they had brought with them. Then he turned the lamp down low, in preparation for the arrival of the lookout. They had already decided that the best way to capture him was to wait in the cabin until he arrived at the end of his spell of duty. But first, they had to provide something which would give him the impression, as he came up to the shack in the dark, that the prisoner was still hanging from the pole.

Using two of the bedrolls and some rope they fashioned a dummy which should fool the look-out provided that, as expected, he went straight in to join the others. They suspended the dummy from the pole and returned to the shack.

Sitting down inside, they talked, keeping their voices low so as not to be overheard by the prisoners. Roy told Will about Anne's concern for his safety and said that she was just about to organize a search for him when Roy arrived.

'I reckon she's taken a shine to you,' said Roy. 'She sure is a fine looking lady. Some folks have all the luck.'

'I'm hoping you're right,' said Will. 'I aim to get a lot better acquainted when we get back to Laringo.'

They settled down to wait for the arrival of the look-out, and just over half an hour later they heard the faint sound of a cough as he approached the shack. They both moved to a position which would be behind the door when it was opened. As Jackson stepped inside, closing the door behind him, Will stepped up and jabbed the end of his gun barrel into the side of the outlaw's neck, while Roy took his gun. Then Jackson was ordered to lie face down on the floor with the others, and his hands and feet were tied.

Since they did not know when Luke Brent

was due back, or how many men he would have with him, they decided that the prisoners be moved to Laringo as early as possible. One by one, their hands and feet were untied, and they were ordered on to their horses. Then their hands were tied behind them. Roy collected his horse from outside the ravine, and he and Will led the four prisoners towards Laringo.

When they were approaching the outskirts of town they halted, and Will checked the ropes round the prisoners' wrists, after ordering them to dismount and lie face down on the ground.

'I'll go on ahead, Roy,' he said, 'just like we planned. I won't be long. Keep a close watch on these four, and use your six-gun if anybody tries anything foolish.'

He went on alone, and rode behind the buildings until he reached the rear of the telegraph office. He dismounted and walked round to the front. As he entered, Frost, in the middle of transmitting a message, turned his head to see who had come in. He froze as he recognized Will and saw the Peacemaker in his hand. There was a gun in the drawer in front of him, but he decided it would be foolhardy to go for it. Will took him, at gunpoint, through the rear door of the livery stable, where Mason happened to be in conversation with two Texas Rangers called Parton and Rooney. They had called in briefly at Laringo, on their way to Amarillo.

When Will and his prisoner entered, Mason had just finished telling the rangers about the disappearance of Will and the departure of Roy to search for him. Surprised and relieved, he greeted Will and introduced him to the rangers, who looked curiously at Frost.

'We heard about you going after Luke Brent,' said Parton. 'Who's this man with you?'

'This is Frost, the telegraph operator and Wells Fargo agent in town,' Will replied. 'He's been passing information and messages to the Curtis gang. They have a hideout about fourteen miles east of here, and Luke Brent's joined up with them.'

'This is real interesting,' said Parton. 'We want Curtis just as much as we want Brent.'

'As far as Curtis is concerned,' said Will, 'my friend Roy is holding him and three of his men prisoner just outside town. And another two of his men are buried in the cemetery here. The bad news is that Brent's still on the loose. He's away somewhere, recruiting more members for the gang. Don't know when he's due back.'

Astonished, the two rangers stared at Will.

'This is great news,' said Parton. 'My partner here will take care of Frost. I'll come with you to bring the prisoners in. Then we'll take them all into Amarillo.'

As Will and the ranger rode off, Mason hurried to the doctor's house. Anne answered his knock. He knew that she had been waiting, with increasing anxiety, for news of Will.

'It's good news, Anne,' he said. 'Will's back safe with some prisoners, and Roy's with him. They'll be bringing them into town shortly.'

Anne went outside and it was not long before she saw the approaching group of riders. As they drew near, Will broke away, then stopped by her. She smiled up at him.

'Good to see you again,' she said. 'We'd pretty near given you up.'

'It's good to be back,' said Will. 'For a while there, I figured I'd never have the chance of seeing you again. Just now, I've got to go along to the livery stable, but I'd like to see you later, and tell you what's happened.'

'I'll be waiting,' she said.

Will went along to the stable, where all the prisoners, including Frost, had been assembled inside. Parton took him aside.

'The liveryman's agreed to let us keep these prisoners in the stable overnight,' he said. 'Then we'll take them to Amarillo tomorrow. We've identified Curtis and three of his gang, Tobin, Jackson and Lester. We've seen pictures of them all. This is a real good haul. But I'm sorry Brent ain't with them. You figure to stay on his trail?'

'Maybe Roy and me will ride out to the hide-out in the morning and wait around there a while in case Brent comes back,' said Will. 'But about tonight. D'you want any help guarding the prisoners?'

'No thanks,' Parton replied. 'We'll both stay in the stable, and take turns guarding them.'

Will had a few words with Roy, and it was agreed that they would ride out to the hide-out the following morning, and keep it under observation from cover, in the hope that Brent would return. Then Will went to see Anne, and they were joined by her brother.

Will told them what had happened at the hide-out, saying that Brent was not among the prisoners captured. He said he intended to return there with Roy the following day. If there was no sign of Brent during the next few days, they would come back to Laringo.

When Will had left, the doctor sensed that his sister was deeply worried. He asked her why.

'For a while there,' she said, 'I thought it was all over, and there was no more danger for Will to face. Now I'm back to worrying again.'

ELEVEN

Luke Brent reached his destination late in the evening, and found Wilson sitting in a poker game in the saloon. The gambler was a tall, slim man with a long, hard face. He was neatly dressed in black. He carried a pearl-handled Colt .45 revolver in a right-hand holster, and a derringer pistol concealed inside his clothing. Although a crooked gambler, and occasional robber, he had not yet been identified as a criminal by the law.

He showed no sign of recognition as he saw Brent come in, walk up to the bar, and order a beer. But five minutes later, he pulled out of the game and on his way out passed just behind Brent, who was standing alone. As he did so, he gave him the number of his hotel room. Five minutes later, Brent left and walked over to the hotel. The lobby was deserted. He went up to Wilson's room, and the gambler let him in.

They sat down, and Brent explained the operation that was being planned, emphasising the high likely value of Wilson's share of the proceeds.

'As a matter of fact,' said the gambler, 'I was thinking of moving on. I ain't been doing too well lately. When d'you want me?'

'Tomorrow,' Brent replied. 'I figured we could leave here in the morning.'

Wilson agreed to this, and Brent took a room at the hotel. The following morning they left after an early breakfast, and arrived at the ravine around noon. Brent's first inkling that something was wrong came when there was no challenge from the lookout. Cautiously, the two men rode into the ravine and up to the shack. There was no sign of the Curtis gang or the prisoner. All the horses were gone.

'Either the law's picked them up,' said Brent, 'or Curtis got wind of the law heading this way, and they all lit out, taking Drummond with them.'

'What do we do now, then?' asked Wilson.

'We'll head for Laringo,' said Brent. 'Maybe they've been taken there. Nobody knows you there, so you can ride in on your own and find out if anything's known in town about what's happened here. I'll stay outside of town myself.'

The two men rode towards Laringo. They met or saw nobody until they were just in sight of town, when they saw a buckboard approaching them. It was driven by a homesteader called Slater. They stopped just before he reached them, and he pulled up.

'Howdy,' said Brent. 'That place we can just see ahead. Would that be Laringo?'

'It sure is,' said Slater, a naturally loquacious man. 'Just come from there myself. Went in to pick up some supplies and see Doc Kincaid. But he's just left for Amarillo for some kind of conference tomorrow. You going into Laringo? If you are, you'll be hearing all about the capture of the Curtis gang.'

'I've heard about them,' said Brent. 'It's time they were picked up. Where were they caught?'

'In a hide-out east of here,' the homesteader replied. 'Four of them. And the rangers are holding Frost, the telegraph operator, as well. Seems he was in cahoots with the gang. They're holding them all in the livery stable till tomorrow, with the two rangers guarding them.'

'So the rangers caught up with them,' said Wilson.

'Not exactly,' said Slater. 'They were brought into town by a man called Drummond and a friend of his. The two rangers just happened to be in town at the time, so they took over the guarding of them in the livery stable till tomorrow. Then they'll be taken to Amarillo.'

They left the homesteader and rode on for a short distance while digesting the news. Then they stopped to talk.

'We've got to try and rescue them,' said Brent. 'Otherwise I'm on my own. And you can guess how long it would take me to find enough good men to make up another gang like the one I had before.'

'Just a minute!' said Wilson. 'I took on to help out in a robbery, not to free prisoners from the law.'

'I can guarantee,' said Brent, 'that Curtis would pay a high price for his freedom, and I'm willing to chip in myself.'

'What plan d'you have in mind?' asked Wilson.

'The time to free them is tonight,' said Brent. 'It was a stroke of luck, getting that information from the homesteader. We'll set up some sort of diversion in town, and surprise the two rangers guarding the prisoners in the livery stable. You'd better ride into town alone when we've talked the plan over. See if you can get any more information, and try and get a look inside the stable. Then come back to me. We'll both ride in later, after dark.'

After the two men had settled on a plan, Wilson prepared to leave. As he was riding off, Brent called out to him.

'Don't forget to check the doctor's house,' he said.

When Wilson reached Laringo he rode straight to the livery stable, dismounted, and went inside. Near the back of the stable, the liveryman was speaking to a Texas Ranger. He walked up to them, and spoke to Mason. He could see no sign of the prisoners, but guessed that they were lying in an empty stall at the back of the stable. Six stalls were occupied by horses.

'Howdy,' he said, noticing the four gunbelts and six-guns lying on the floor near the ranger. 'Can you feed and water my horse? I aim to leave for Amarillo in an hour or so.'

'Sure,' said Mason, and Wilson left the stable. The ranger, who had been keenly observing him, put him down as a professional gambler.

Wilson walked along the street until he came to the doctor's house, marked by the shingle outside. He walked up to the door, stood in a small porch, and knocked on the door repeatedly. There was no answer. Unobserved, he walked round to the back and inspected the door and window. Then he walked along, past the rear of the livery stable, before returning to the street. As far as he knew, his movements behind the buildings had not been observed. He went into the saloon, and had a drink at the bar. The customers were still talking about the capture of the outlaws, but he learnt nothing of importance to add to what he already knew. After a while, he returned to the stable, and Mason brought his horse out.

'I heard in the saloon about the prisoners you've got in there,' said Wilson. 'It's sure good to hear that the law's caught up with them at last.'

Fifteen minutes after Wilson rode out of town, Anne returned to the house after a visit to see the liveryman's wife, a close friend of hers.

When Wilson reached Brent, in hiding outside town, he told him what he had seen in Laringo.

'Those weapons and horses inside the stable are just what we need,' said Brent, 'and now we know the doctor's house is empty, we can use it like we planned. We'll ride in after midnight.'

In Laringo, not long after the departure of Wilson, Will and Roy went along to the stable, and offered to keep a watch, in turn, outside the stable, during the night, in case a rescue attempt was launched by friends of the prisoners. They also said that they were willing to ride to Amarillo with the rangers on the following day, to help guard the prisoners on the way. Both the offers were gladly accepted, and it was arranged that during the forthcoming night Roy would cover the period until midnight, when he would be relieved by Will until four o'clock. Will then left Roy and went to see Anne. He figured that the time had come for a serious talk with her. She led him into the living-room and they both sat down.

'I've been thinking a lot about us lately, Anne,' he said, 'and it just hit me today that without you around I'd be a very lonely man. Up to now I've been thinking mostly of capturing Brent, but that don't seem so important now, and I'm giving up the chase. The law will catch up with him one day. What's important to me now is trying to persuade you to marry me so that we can spend the rest of our lives together.'

She smiled at him. 'What made you think

I'd need any persuading?' she asked. 'I was mighty grateful for what you did at the Sinclair homestead, but even without that I knew right away that you were the man for me. I've been waiting quite a spell for the right one to come along.'

'So,' said Will, relieved and happy, 'we can set the date for the wedding. How's your brother going to take this?'

'Andrew's a good brother,' she replied. 'He'll be happy for me. He'll miss my help, maybe, but plenty of doctors out here manage pretty well on their own.'

'Roy and me are helping the rangers take the prisoners to Amarillo tomorrow,' said Will. 'When I get back we'll fix a date for the wedding. And we've got to decide on our plans for the future.'

'Have you anything in mind?' she asked.

'It has to be something we both agree on,' said Will, 'but I did have one idea. There's a valley in Wyoming where I have some friends who'd be real pleased to meet up with you. I thought of buying some land there and running a small cattle ranch. It's mighty nice country up there, and a great place to bring up a family. How does the idea strike you?'

'It sounds pretty good to me,' she said,

'and a lot better than being a lawman's wife. I was thinking that maybe that's what you wanted to do. We'll talk more about it when you get back from Amarillo.'

It was now dark outside, and a little later Will left Anne and went to his hotel room for a short rest before relieving Roy at midnight. Anne went up to her bedroom at the rear of the house shortly after ten o'clock. Her brother normally slept in a room immediately below hers, on the ground floor. Happy after her talk with Will, she remained awake for a short while, thinking about the forthcoming wedding, then drifted off into a dreamless sleep.

Half an hour after Will relieved Roy outside the stable, which was some way from the doctor's house, Brent and Wilson rode up to the remains of an old abandoned shack just outside town, and tethered their horses. Then they walked behind the buildings to the rear of the doctor's house, which was in darkness. Wilson pointed out the flimsy back door he had noticed earlier in the day. Brent threw his weight against it, and at his second attempt the lock broke and the door swung open. They went inside and, with the help of matches, they collected three oil lamps on the ground floor. They went into the living-room, and sat down near the foot of the stairs leading to Anne's bedroom.

Upstairs, Anne stirred in her sleep at the first impact of Brent's body on the door. Then, as the door was forced open, she was instantly awake. She heard the sounds of movements down below. Quietly, she left her room, and walked halfway down the stairs. There was no light down below, and she could hear two men talking. The voices were not familiar, and she was sure that the intruders must be there with criminal intent. She moved a little further down to see if she could hear what was being said. Then she heard a man speak, close to the foot of the stairs.

'Hand me some matches, Luke,' he said, 'and I'll take a look round upstairs.'

One of the men, thought Anne, with rising panic, could be Luke Brent, the murderer of Will's brother, though she could not understand why they had broken into the house. Hastily, she returned to her bedroom, tidied the bedclothes, and stepped inside a large wardrobe. She had barely closed the door behind her when Wilson entered the room, struck another match, and walked round it before going downstairs. She decided to stay where she was until she could be sure that the intruders had left. She sat down sideways inside the wardrobe, straining her ears for any sounds from below.

Brent and Wilson poured the oil from the lamps around the floors of the living-room and kitchen, then ignited it. Their intention was to go and wait behind the stable until the burning house had drawn everyone's attention. Then they would deal with the two rangers.

Will, who happened at the time to be walking along the side of the stable remote from the doctor's house, towards the rear, heard the faint sound as Brent's foot struck a stone embedded in the ground, and he stumbled, cursed, and almost fell. Will moved to the corner, drawing his Peacemaker. Looking round it, he could see two figures approaching. As he challenged them they both opened fire. Will hit Wilson with his first shot, and the gambler went down. Will drew back as a bullet from Brent's gun hit the wall close to his head. Brent turned, crouched down, and ran off into the darkness towards his horse. When Will risked another look round the corner, the outlaw was not in sight.

Will ran up to the man lying on the ground and picked up his gun. Then he checked him over, to find that he was dead. He started back to speak to the ranger on guard inside the stable. Parton had come to the main entrance on hearing the shots outside, and Will called out to him as he approached. He told him and Ranger Rooney what had happened, then went back and dragged Wilson inside the stable. Parton lit a lamp, and the three men looked at the dead man's face. They were joined by Mason, who had heard the shooting.

'He's a stranger to me,' said Will, and the others all said that the man was unknown to them.

'I'm wondering who it is that got away,' said Will. 'He'll be long gone by now.'

Suddenly, they heard the sound of running feet on the street outside, and the hotel owner appeared in the doorway.

'It's the doc's house,' he shouted. 'It's on fire. We need every man we can get. And I ain't seen the doc's sister. I don't know whether she's inside or not.'

Mason and the hotel owner ran off to rouse as many men as possible to fight the fire. Will, desperately concerned about Anne's safety, ran as fast as he could to the burning house. As he approached he could see the flames rising inside. There was no sign of Anne. He ran to the front door. It was stoutly built, and firmly locked. He ran round to the back, and found the rear door open. The fire had taken a firm hold, and flames and dense smoke were rising inside. With his bandanna tied over his nose and mouth, Will ran through the door into the burning building.

In the wardrobe inside her bedroom, Anne had heard the two men moving about as they scattered the oil. But she was unaware of the fire which had been started down below until the smoke came billowing up the stairs through the open door of her bedroom and seeped into the wardrobe. She started to cough, then stood up, pushed the wardrobe door open, and stepped out. The smoke was dense, and before she could make a move in an effort to escape from the building, she collapsed on the floor in a paroxysm of coughing.

At this moment Will ran up the stairs and into the bedroom. Guided by the sound of her coughing, he found Anne on the floor. He judged that if he moved quickly there was still time to get her out of the building by way of the stairs. He took a blanket off the bed and wrapped it completely around her. He draped another one over his head, picked

Anne up and moved quickly down the stairs and out of the house. Moving well away from the burning building, he laid Anne on the ground and threw the two smouldering blankets aside. She continued coughing for a while, as a number of townspeople ran up and started to follow a previously rehearsed plan for dealing with building fires.

When the fit of coughing had subsided, and Anne was breathing easier, Mason's wife came up and insisted that she be taken to her place to recover. Will carried her to the liveryman's house, and up to a bedroom. Then, at Anne's suggestion, he ran back to help fight the fire.

When Will reached the burning house he found the fire well under control, and it was not long before the flames were extinguished. There was some damage to furniture and flooring downstairs, and to the lower half of the stairs. But the upper floor was not affected, and fortunately, the annexe which the doctor used for seeing patients and keeping his medicines and files, had remained unscathed. Will took the good news back to Anne.

The following morning Anne was feeling much better when Will called after breakfast to see her. While he was there Ranger Parton came in to see him.

'There's no need for you to ride with us to Amarillo to help guard the prisoners,' he said. 'A ranger has just rode in on his way back there. He'll go along with us and your friend Roy Dillon. But you'll be needed at the trial. That's likely to be pretty soon. We'll let you know the date by telegraph. We'll be leaving shortly.'

Will left with Parton to see Roy and thank him before he left.

'We're expecting you for the wedding,' he said.

By the afternoon of the following day, when her brother returned, Anne, who had suffered no burns, was almost back to normal. When he had recovered from the shock of seeing the damage to the house, she told him of the wedding plans. He was genuinely happy for her, and wished them both well.

The following day Andrew, with the help of Will and some of the townsfolk, started work on the house to make it habitable. By the end of the day after that the doctor and his sister were able to move back in.

The following morning, Will went to see Anne.

'So long as I'm here,' he said, 'I'll ride out

with you if you need to visit one of the homesteads. But after all that's been happening around here, I'm worried about you driving out of town alone while I'm away at the trial. I got this at the store, and I'd like you to carry it if you leave town.'

He showed her a Colt .41 pocket revolver with a 2¼-inch barrel.

'That skirt you wear when you go out in the buggy,' he said. 'Maybe you could fix a small pocket in that to hide this in. And I could take you out and spend an hour or two today showing you how to use it. I sure would be a lot happier if I knew you were wearing it.'

'In that case,' said Anne, 'let's do it. I'll sew the pocket in today.'

The following morning a settler called Nelson came to the doctor's house. He told how his wife had a badly twisted ankle which prevented her from walking. He asked if the doctor would call and see her. Andrew had several other patients to attend to that day and he asked Anne if she could go to the Nelson homestead with some special bandaging, and take a look at the injury for him. Anne told Nelson that she and Will would drive out to the homestead in the buggy two or three hours later.

When Luke Brent fled from the rear of the livery stable in Laringo, he collected his horse, and rode out to a grove of trees where he had been hiding. His initial impulse had been to flee the area immediately, but then he decided that before he left he must rid himself once and for all of the man who had been responsible for the defeat of his father and himself in Wyoming, and who now, he suspected, was bent on his capture. He laid low in the grove for the next two days. Then he decided to try and find out, with minimum risk to himself, what was going on in Laringo.

He had noticed a solitary homestead, not far from where he was hiding, and decided to pay it a visit.

When he reached it, he dismounted and knocked on the door. It was opened by Nelson. He asked him for directions to Laringo, adding that he was looking for a friend of his called Will Drummond.

'Well I'm darned,' said Nelson. 'If you wait here an hour or so, he'll be turning up with the doctor's sister. Did you know he was fixing to marry her?'

Brent shook his head, and the homesteader invited him inside to meet his wife, who was sitting in the living-room. Then he gave him all the news about Will's involvement in the capture of the Curtis gang, and the intention of the couple to marry after the trial.

'That's mighty interesting,' said Brent, and drew his revolver. 'It so happens I have a score to settle with Drummond, and I don't want you two interfering when he turns up.'

Keeping them covered, he opened a door at the back of the room and looked inside. It was a small storeroom, with no weapons visible. He ordered Nelson and his wife, supported by her husband, inside.

'Either of you make a noise,' he said, 'and I'll kill the two of you.'

He closed the door, and dragged a heavy chest in front of it. Then he led his horse into the barn, and returned to the house, where he sat at a window, awaiting the arrival of Will and his companion. Just under an hour had passed before he saw them approaching. He drew back and watched as they climbed down from the buggy, and walked up to the door together, When Anne knocked on the door he opened it, but kept behind it as he pulled it towards him.

As Anne stepped inside, Brent grabbed

her arm and held his pistol against her head. She froze. Will, shocked to see Brent, and aware of the danger to Anne, also stayed motionless. The outlaw ordered Will to drop his six-gun on the floor. He checked him for additional weapons, then ordered them to sit on the floor, side by side, with their backs to the wall. Anne was sitting with Will on her left. Brent pulled up a chair and sat down facing them.

'Time for a talk,' he said. 'I'm curious about why you've been chasing me like this, Drummond,' said the outlaw. 'Maybe you'd like to tell me the reason.'

'Why not,' said Will. 'You tortured and murdered my brother Clint when he was a lawman in Kansas.'

'So that's it,' said Brent. 'I hadn't figured you were his brother. Don't remember a lot about it. You've got to understand I don't like lawmen. Any chance to get rid of one, I take. As for you two, I aim to shoot you right here and now, Drummond. The lady can stay alive for another half-hour. That should be long enough.'

Anne was wearing the full skirt into which, being left-handed, she had sewn, on the left side, the pocket for the small revolver. She had told Will that she was taking it along to get some more practice on the way back. On sitting down she pulled her skirt sideways so as to cover Will's right hand, as well as her left one. While Brent was talking, she was surreptitiously manoeuvring the small revolver out of the pocket in her skirt.

As the outlaw finished speaking, she slipped the pistol into Will's hand. He coughed to drown the sound as he pulled the hammer back. Just as he had done this, Brent pointed his six-gun at Will's head and started to pull the hammer back with his thumb. But before he had finished the movement, Will brought his pistol into view and shot the outlaw in the head, instantly killing him. Brent fell off the chair onto the floor as Anne and Will rose to their feet.

Will, who had noticed the chest against the door, moved it away so that the couple in the storeroom could come out. Then, while Anne tended to Mrs Nelson, her husband and Will took the dead outlaw into the barn. On returning to Laringo, Will arranged for the body to be picked up.

Will attended the trial two days later. Curtis and his men were all sentenced to be hanged. Frost was given a long prison sentence.

Two weeks later Will and Anne were

married, and two days after that they left Laringo for the valley in Wyoming where Will had so soundly thwarted the evil plans of Eli Brent, aided by his son Luke. There, among friends, they set up a small cattle ranch, and started to raise a family.